MR. PERFECT

Randi took a deep breath and tried not to blush as the laughter died down in the classroom. Then, to her dismay, the boy sitting in front of her slowly turned around. It was Ned Taggert, one of the cutest boys in school, and he had the strangest expression on his face. As he continued to stare at Randi intently, she felt like she wanted to die.

Ned Taggert was everything Randi wished she could be—popular, confident, self-assured. Ned was a star at Brockenborough Prep. He was president of the student council, captain of the debate team and a varsity letterman in three sports. The list of his accomplishments went on and on. And if all that wasn't enough, he was also unbelievably cute—tall, with blue eyes and short, sandy-blond hair. Kind of rugged-looking in a cool way. Randi knew there wasn't a girl in the room who wasn't dying to go out with him. *He's Mister Perfect,* she thought. *And he's also completely out of my league.*

BANTAM SWEET DREAMS ROMANCES

Mr. Perfect

Stefanie Curtis

BANTAM BOOKS
TORONTO • NEW YORK • LONDON • SYDNEY • AUCKLAND

RL 6, IL age 11 and up

MR. PERFECT
A Bantam Book/June 1990

ISBN 0-553-27553-4

Published simultaneously in the United States and Canada

*Bantam Books are published by Bantam Books, a division of
Bantam Doubleday Dell Publishing Group, Inc. Its trademark,
consisting of the words "Bantam Books" and the portrayal of a
rooster, is Registered in U.S. Patent and Trademark Office and
in other countries. Marca Registrada. Bantam Books, Inc., 666 Fifth
Avenue, New York, New York 10103.*

Printed and bound in Great Britain by
Cox & Wyman Ltd., Reading

For
Bonnie Stokes

Chapter One

The moment Randi had been dreading finally arrived.

Her English teacher, Mr. Harvey, slowly turned to her with an unmistakable look in his eye. He was about to call on her, there was no doubt about it. "Now, class, I'd like you to turn to page one forty-six, the beginning of chapter twenty-four," he began. "Ms. Hinton," he said to Randi, "would you read the first paragraph aloud, please?"

Randi stood up miserably. Already her hands felt a little clammy, and her face was burning. She *hated* reading aloud in front of the class. After a short, nervous swallow, she turned her eyes to her text, Jane Austen's *Pride and Prejudice*.

"Miss B-B-Bingley's letter arrived . . ." Randi began shakily, and the boy next to her muffled a laugh. ". . . and p-put an end to . . ." Randi felt herself turn beet red. What was the matter with her? Why did she always start stuttering like this when she had to speak in front of a group?

"Go on," Mr. Harvey prompted. Someone else snickered behind her.

". . . and put an end to doubt," Randi plunged on, biting down on each word. "The very first s-s-s . . ." She paused, feeling defeated. She wanted to cry out in sheer frustration.

"The very first sentence . . ." Mr. Harvey coached her, sounding sorry he had asked her to read in the first place.

Randi took a deep breath, trying to collect herself. Then, to her dismay, the boy sitting in front of her slowly turned around. It was Ned Taggert, one of the cutest boys in the school, and he had the strangest expression on his face. He continued to stare at Randi intently. Randi wanted to die.

"Uh, thank you, Ms. Hinton," Mr. Harvey said kindly. "You may sit down. Now, can anyone tell me what Jane Austen is doing here?"

Randi sank into her chair, wishing she

could disappear. Even though Ned Taggert had turned back to face the front, Randi thought she could see his shoulders shaking as he stifled a laugh. *I hate you, Ned Taggert*, she thought. But deep down she knew this wasn't true.

Ned Taggert was everything Randi wished she could be—popular, confident, self-assured. Ned was a star at Brockenborough Prep. He was president of the student council, captain of the debate team, a varsity letterman in three sports. The list of his accomplishments went on and on. If all that wasn't enough, he was unbelievably cute—tall, with blue eyes and short, sandy-blond hair. Kind of rugged-looking in a cool way, Randi thought. There wasn't a girl in the room who wouldn't go out with him. He was Mister Perfect. Randi sighed. He was also completely out of her league.

Randi tried to turn her attention back to what Mr. Harvey was saying, but it was no use. Gradually her thoughts had turned to another subject, and something far more troubling than Ned Taggert: her upcoming class speech.

Everyone in the Upper School at Brockenborough Prep had to give a speech once a year in front of the entire student body during assembly. Even though it was a short speech, just the thought made Randi shudder. How could she give a speech in front of the whole school when she couldn't even read a paragraph of *Pride and Prejudice* without freezing up?

When the bell rang, Randi flew out of her chair, hoping to make a quick exit, but Brenda Chen caught up with her. "Headed home?" Brenda asked.

Randi nodded mutely. She didn't feel much like talking to anyone.

"I'll walk with you," Brenda persisted. It was obvious that she was only trying to be nice, so Randi reluctantly agreed. Besides, Brenda lived right on her street, so they'd end up walking the same way anyway.

They left the classroom and walked down the long, oak-paneled corridor that ran the length of Monroe Hall, Brockenborough Prep's main building. Like all the other structures on campus, Monroe Hall was very grand, very old, and very well preserved. It seemed more like a mansion or a museum than a school building to Randi. But then, everything about BP impressed her. It was considered the finest prep school in the state, and every now and then Randi felt like pinching herself to make sure she really was a student there and wasn't just dreaming.

As Randi and Brenda made their way out of the big double doors and down the broad flight of steps that led the way outside, two boys from their English class hurried by. "So long, R-R-Randi," one of them murmured, and the other boy burst out laughing. Randi could feel herself turning red all over again.

"Don't pay any attention to them," Brenda told her. "They are *so* juvenile."

"I know," Randi said weakly.

"They're enough to make anybody stutter . . ." Brenda began, then paused uncertainly, as if she had said the wrong thing.

Randi hesitated. Even though she liked Brenda, they weren't close enough to share any secrets. Randi's best friend, Amy Bishop, was the only person she could truly open up to. She could talk to Amy about anything.

Brenda tactfully changed the subject. "So, what are you doing for Thanksgiving?" she asked.

"It's going to be kind of quiet this year," Randi said, flipping her long blonde hair over one shoulder. "Just my mom and me."

"We're going to my grandfather's," Brenda replied. "There's going to be about thirty people there."

"You're lucky," Randi said wistfully.

"No, *you* are," Brenda said. "With all the

kids in my family, holiday gatherings look like parties at Pee Wee's Playhouse."

Randi laughed. And as Brenda launched into a description of her last family dinner, Randi managed to forget about her class speech—and Ned Taggert—for the rest of the walk home.

Randi stared into the mirror and inspected the left side of her face. Then she turned to look at herself from the other angle. Satisfied that her blush was on evenly, she studied her eye makeup. The light lavender shadow she wore brought out her soft green eyes, but she hoped she hadn't overdone it; it was always so hard to tell in the fluorescent bathroom light.

It was Thanksgiving Day, and Randi wanted to look her best. That morning while she was helping her mother prepare the turkey, they had decided to get dressed up for dinner. It was a nice idea, Randi decided. Even though it would be just the two of them, wearing something extra pretty somehow made the occasion seem more special.

Carefully inspecting the outfit she had chosen, a black velvet minidress trimmed with ivory lace, Randi decided she was ready, and after a spray of perfume behind her ears, she left her bedroom. Her mother was already waiting for her in the dining room, looking elegant in an emerald green dress. Her mother had had it for a few years, but it still looked up-to-date and sophisticated. It was one of Randi's favorites. "You look terrific, Mom," Randi breathed.

"Not as terrific as you, sweetie," her mother replied fondly, looking her over. "Oh, dear," she said, blinking back a sudden tear, "where have all the years gone? My baby looks so grown up! And so pretty."

Randi grinned and gave her mom a fierce hug. "The turkey smells delicious."

"It does, doesn't it?" her mother replied as they took their seats at the table. Mrs. Hinton picked up the carving knife. "By the way, I forgot to tell you earlier, I've invited Charles over for dessert."

"Oh." Charles Payne was the man her mother was dating.

Mrs. Hinton's hands froze over the turkey. "Sweetheart," she said quickly, "you don't mind, do you? I thought you liked Charles."

"I do," Randi replied in a small voice.

"Well, you don't seem too happy that he's coming over. I can see it on your face."

"Really, it's okay." Randi tried to force her features into a calm, relaxed expression. "*Really*."

The fact was, she *did* like Charles Payne. He was a friendly man, always very kind to her. It was just hard to accept the fact that he was going out with her mother. No matter how hard she tried, Randi just couldn't get used to the idea. She barely remembered her father, who had died when she was six years old. Her mother had never dated anyone after that—not until Charles Payne appeared on the scene, several months ago. Even though Randi realized it wasn't fair to expect her mother to be a widow forever, she still hadn't accepted the idea of Charles completely. That, she knew, would have to come with time.

"Charles really likes you," her mother went on in a soothing tone. "Why, just the other day—"

"It's okay, Mom," Randi cut in, trying to sound convincing. Still, it hurt a little to think that her mother had gotten dressed up today for someone besides her.

Mrs. Hinton began to carve the turkey. "I ran into Amy's mother the other day in the mall," she said conversationally. "She tells me there's going to be a big Christmas dance at school."

"Uh, yeah, the week before Christmas," Randi said, relieved to leave the subject of Charles behind. "Amy and I are going to be on one of the committees."

"I wish I could afford to buy you a new dress," her mother said with a slight frown. "But with the holidays coming, and money so tight . . ."

"I was going to wear this." Randi gestured at her black velvet dress with a reassuring smile. New dresses, she knew, were a luxury they couldn't afford. Her mother struggled hard to support them, working all day as an executive secretary and then going to school at night to get her real estate license.

"That dress does look lovely on you," Mrs. Hinton admitted, "but I wish I could get you something new, something absolutely fabulous."

"I like this dress, Mom," Randi said softly, moved by her mother's concern. All at once, she felt terribly guilty. It was so obvious how much her mom loved her. How could she be so mean? How could she feel jealous about Charles? Randi reached over the table and squeezed her mother's hand. "It's okay. Really."

"Well, maybe Santa Claus will surprise us both," her mother said, her brown eyes twinkling.

Randi felt a surge of love. "And, Mom, it's okay about Charles too," she added quickly.

"I appreciate your saying that, honey," her mother replied. "Well, I guess we have something else to be thankful for today." She grinned at Randi, who was smiling back.

The doorbell rang just as they were clearing the table, and Randi got up to answer it, smoothing her dress out as she went. Pausing by the oval mirror next to the front door, she inspected her hair, tucking a long blonde strand behind her ear. Much as she hated to admit it, she wanted to look nice for Charles. Secretly she wanted him to like her.

When she swung the door open, she was surprised to find him wearing an elegant black suit, a white shirt, and a bright red tie. She had never seen him so dressed up before, and she had to admit he looked very handsome. A retired baseball player, Charles was a tall yet graceful man, in good shape for his age, which she guessed was around forty.

"Happy Thanksgiving, Randi," he said, flashing her a wide grin. "For you," he added, presenting her with a bouquet of daisies that he had hidden behind his back.

"Th-thanks," Randi managed to say, mortified that she was stammering. With a superhuman effort, she got herself under control. "They're very pretty," she said, taking the flowers and breathing in their soft fragrance.

Then there was a long, awkward pause as Charles looked at her expectantly. "Oh!" Randi exclaimed, reddening. "Come in." *What is there to be so nervous about?* she wondered.

She led him into the dining room, where her mother was arranging a large pumpkin pie and a bowl of whipped cream on the table. "Happy Thanksgiving, Charles," Mrs. Hinton said. Randi noticed that her mother sounded different when she talked to him. Almost like she was flirting.

"Paula," Charles murmured. After giving her a discreet kiss on the cheek, he produced a large bouquet of chrysanthemums and zinnias. Mrs. Hinton's eyes lit up, and Randi suddenly felt embarrassed.

Her mother seated Charles at the head of the dining room table, and as she served the pie, Charles turned to Randi. "So, how's BP?" he asked. Charles had gone to Brockenborough Prep years before.

"School's fine," Randi said shyly. "A lot of work, you know." She racked her brain to think of something else to say, but nothing came to mind.

"Lots of parties coming up for the holidays, I'll bet," Charles went on.

"There's a big dance before Christmas," Mrs. Hinton cut in, seeming to sense her daughter's nervousness. "We were just talking about it—"

Her words were interrupted by the telephone ringing. "Randi, would you serve the pie while

I get that?" she asked. "Help yourself to some whipped cream," she told Charles, then disappeared into the kitchen.

"Looks delicious," Charles said as Randi placed a thick wedge in front of him.

Randi nodded, thinking desperately for something to say. "Mom made it this afternoon," she quickly added, trying to keep up her end of the conversation.

"Randi!" her mother's voice called out. "It's for you." With an undeniable feeling of relief, Randi excused herself and went into the kitchen.

"Here she is now," her mother was saying into the phone. "Thank you. You, too, dear." She handed Randi the receiver. "Amy," she said as she headed back out to the dining room.

"Hiya," Randi greeted her best friend. They hadn't spoken yet that day, which was unusual.

"Happy Turkey Day," Amy said with a giggle. "Are you *stuffed?*"

Randi groaned. "Um-hmm. How about you?"

"I've managed to leave some room for dessert, which is why I called. Would you and your mom like to come over and have dessert with us?" Amy asked.

"I wish we could," Randi said, "but we

can't. We have company," she added in a stage whisper.

"Charles?" Amy guessed. There was nothing about Randi's life that Amy didn't know.

"Uh-huh."

"Really? It sounds like things are getting pretty serious between your mom and him," Amy observed. "I mean, Thanksgiving *is* a family holiday and all."

"I guess so," Randi hedged feebly.

Amy read the hesitation in her voice instantly. "*Randi!* We've been over this a zillion times. Charles is a nice man."

"I know."

"Besides, I think he's cute." Amy had met Charles the month before, when she was spending the night at the Hintons'.

"Maybe, but he's not *your* potential stepfather," Randi countered.

"Your mom could do a lot worse," Amy persisted, then changed the subject abruptly. "Is there any chance that you could come over for dessert by yourself?"

Randi thought for a moment. Amy's dad, Ford Bishop, was one of the wealthiest men in town, and Randi thought of their enormous house and the grand dining room where Thanksgiving dinner was being served. Dessert alone was bound to be an extravagant affair. It *was* tempting. "I can't," she said reluctantly.

"Why not?"

"Because Mom would probably get upset." Randi's voice dropped to a whisper again. "Charles just got here, and I think she wants us to get to know each other and all."

"You make it sound like it's some kind of torture," Amy groaned. "Honest, Randi, there's nothing wrong with him. Give him a chance, okay?"

"All right, I will," Randi agreed halfheartedly. "See you tomorrow?" The two girls arranged to spend the day together, working on their entries for the upcoming student photography contest.

"Positively. Let's meet early," Amy replied. "I've got lots to tell you, and we have lots to do."

"Nine-thirty okay?" Randi suggested.

"Perfect. See you later, alligator."

Randi laughed. "Yeah, see you."

Chapter Two

At exactly nine-thirty the following morning Randi hurried across Brockenborough's town square toward the city park, where she had arranged to meet Amy, her camera slung over her shoulder. It was a crisp, wintry day, and she was full of enthusiasm. Photography was her passion, her absolute favorite thing in the world.

Amy was already waiting for her, standing beneath the statue of the town's founder, Horace Brockenborough. While Randi's equipment consisted of a single 35mm camera on a wide, macraméed strap, her friend was weighed down with two cameras and a large shoulder bag loaded with light meters, filters, and lenses.

But that was Amy, Randi thought. When she did something, she did it all the way.

"Are you sure you brought enough equipment?" Randi teased.

"I think so," Amy replied with a wry smile, tugging at her wavy chestnut hair. "The light right now is so beautiful," she added, looking up at the soft, pale sky.

"Let's get started, then," Randi said eagerly.

"What do you think about old Horace?" Amy asked, nodding at the somber statue behind them.

"I like his hands," Randi said after examining their subject. "They're all gnarly and bony." With that she lifted her camera to her eye and began to inch forward.

The two girls were taking pictures for BP's annual student photography contest, and after much discussion they had decided to photograph the statues that lined the entrance to the park. It had been Randi's idea originally, and Amy immediately liked it. They seemed to agree on all the important things, which was probably why they were best friends.

After examining the statue's hands from several angles, Randi finally snapped two pictures, then Amy, after a lot of complicated maneuvering with her light meter, took a photograph from a different angle. Then Randi took a picture of Amy taking a picture, which broke them both up.

"I have a feeling these are going to turn out great," Randi said expansively, taking in a deep breath of the morning air.

Amy combed her fingers through her hair, which she'd recently had permed. "Hey, I forgot to ask you," she said, looking at Randi with interest, "how did the rest of Thanksgiving with Charles go?"

"All right," Randi sighed. "We sat and talked for a while, and then I excused myself to give them some time alone. It turned out pretty well, I guess."

"You'll never guess who showed up at our house after I talked to you," Amy whispered. Before Randi could answer, Amy exclaimed, "Rusty!"

"You're kidding!" Randi said, her eyes wide. Rusty was Amy's ex-boyfriend. Amy had recently broken up with him for reasons Randi thought were crazy. Rusty was a great guy— and really cute, too.

"Rusty *and* his parents," Amy went on, shaking her head. "It's hard to avoid him when his mother and my mother are best friends."

"I'm surprised he came at all."

"Oh, come on, Randi. I'm sure his mother

made him come. You know his mother and my mother are dying for us to get married someday."

Randi nodded thoughtfully. They had talked about Amy's problems with Rusty many times before. Still, Randi didn't think Amy was being honest with herself. Amy really liked Rusty, Randi was convinced of it. The only reason she had broken up with him at all was to rebel against her family. They liked him, which made him less exciting to Amy. But now she was having second thoughts, Randi was sure of it. "So did you talk to him?" Randi asked.

"A little."

"What about?"

"Umm, nothing much. I just said Happy Thanksgiving and all that. Then he went with my brothers into the den, and they watched football for the rest of the afternoon."

"Did it feel weird to talk to him?"

"Well . . . he did have a funny look in his eyes," she said finally. "Kind of sad."

"I know he wants you back," Randi said quietly. "That's what Bruce Merriweather told me in biology."

"But I don't want him back," Amy said without conviction. "And don't look at me like that," she added.

"Like what?"

"Like I'm crazy or something."

"You are crazy. If you weren't so pigheaded, you and Rusty would be back together," Randi argued. "You just won't give him a chance. And you know I'm right."

Amy considered this for a moment, then squared her shoulders. "You're not right at all. I want to be able to date some other people for a change. I want some freedom. His parents and my parents have been trying to pair us off since we were little kids. Anyway," she added mysteriously, "I heard some gossip that makes me glad I'm single again."

"What?" Randi sat down at the base of the statue and stretched her legs out. This was not the first photo session that had been interrupted by a long talk.

"My brother told me Ned Taggert and Linda Olgeirson broke up last week."

The thought of Ned staring at her during her recitation from *Pride and Prejudice* flashed through Randi's mind. "Ugh. You can have him."

"Are you feeling all right?" Amy asked half-seriously, putting her hand on Randi's forehead to see if she had a fever. "He just happens to be the hottest guy around. Wouldn't you go out with him if he asked you?"

"He doesn't even know my name."

"I'm sure he does," Amy insisted. "Isn't he in your English class? Just because you've never been introduced . . ."

"You can have him," Randi repeated stubbornly as she again recalled the strange look Ned had given her in class the other day. She didn't have a prayer as far as he was concerned, she thought darkly, so it didn't matter. Maybe she was pretty enough, but she certainly didn't think she was cool enough. This was only her second year at Brockenborough Prep, and she still didn't feel like she really fit in. Besides, she had never had a real boyfriend. She had had her fair share of dates, but nobody serious so far. Ned Taggert would never go for a girl like that. He was out of her league.

"What is your problem?" Amy demanded. "Something's bugging you, I can tell. What is it?"

"Nothing." Randi got up and squinted through the lens of her camera, hoping to get off the subject of Ned. It was too upsetting to think about. "Let's get back to work."

"*Tell!*" Amy insisted.

"Well," Randi lowered her camera reluctantly. "It's kind of dumb, but I had this terrible experience in Mr. Harvey's class the other day."

Amy leaned forward, and Randi rapidly filled her in on the details—how nervous she had been when she had to read out loud, how some people snickered under their breath, how Ned had stared at her. When she was finished, Amy was silent for a moment.

"Are you really sure Ned was laughing at you?" she finally asked. "That doesn't sound like him. He seems like a pretty nice guy."

"Well, I'm not exactly sure," Randi admitted. "But the look he gave me was like I was so pitiful—"

"That's all in your mind," Amy cut in. "You've really got to stop thinking that way, Randi. You're a much better person than you think you are. You just need to be a little more positive about yourself!"

"Well . . ." Randi blushed and realized this was yet another example of how nice her friend was—Amy always tried to build up her self-confidence. "Actually, there's something else that's bothering me."

"What?" Amy asked.

"My class speech." She studied a broken branch lying on the ground next to the statue, not wanting to look her friend in the eye.

Amy exhaled with exasperation. "Honestly, Randi," she snorted. "I thought you had a serious problem. Your class speech? You've got to be kidding! It only has to be five minutes long, and it's only once a year. I thought you had a *real* problem."

"It is a real problem to me," Randi said quietly.

"Oh, Randi," Amy said quickly. "I didn't mean to sound so cold about it. But can't you manage to get through just five minutes?"

"It's thinking about it ahead of time that's so bad. It's like, I can do it mentally, but my body refuses to cooperate."

"What do you mean?"

"I mean my hands sweat, I turn red, my heart starts to pound, and then I start to stutter. It's impossible to concentrate when all that's happening to you."

"Have you always had this problem?" Amy asked. "I've never noticed it before."

"Well, it only really happens when I'm in front of a group. And it's kind of getting worse lately," Randi admitted. "My speech is January tenth. Just thinking about it is driving me crazy. It's going to ruin Christmas."

"Have you got a topic yet?"

"No," Randi sighed. "Have you?"

"No, but my speech isn't until the end of March. You should try to come up with an idea soon. Maybe then you'll be able to relax."

"You're right," Randi said, pressing her hand against her temples. "I don't have the slightest idea what to talk about, though."

"Well, you don't have to knock yourself out. Most of the speeches have been so boring that no one listens to them anyway. Did you hear that one Clark Weldon gave last week?"

"About trees indigenous to the greater Brockenborough area?" Randi giggled. "That was a real snore."

"Wait a minute!" Amy exclaimed. "That's it! You should pick a topic so boring that even the faculty falls asleep. If no one's listening to you, there's nothing to be nervous about, right?"

"Well, it does count toward our final English grade," Randi reminded her. "And you know I have to keep my grades up."

Amy nodded. Randi was on an academic scholarship at Brokenborough Prep: It was the only way her mother could afford to send her there. Part of the arrangement was that her grades had to stay above a C+ average. The class speech counted enough toward her final English grade that she couldn't afford to blow it.

Amy got up and stretched. "Well, you should try not to worry about it. We'll get you through this somehow. Just think of a topic, okay? Wait, don't move!" she said in her next breath.

Randi looked at her, puzzled.

"The way the light is hitting you, you look incredible," Amy explained, aiming her camera. "Hold it."

Randi felt a warm feeling rush over her. No matter how bad she felt, Amy always managed to bring a smile to her face.

Around one-thirty they took a break for lunch and headed for the Annex, a popular hangout in the center of town. The place was packed, and they slipped into the only vacant table, a tiny one near the window.

"I'm starved," Randi exclaimed, pulling off her scarf and hat. "What are you going to have?"

But Amy just sat there silently, her brown eyes fixed on something over Randi's shoulder. She looked completely astonished.

"Amy?" Randi demanded, "what is it?"

When Amy still didn't answer, Randi subtly swiveled her head to follow her friend's gaze. There, in a booth several tables behind them, was Rusty. Sitting next to him was Gwen Davis, BP's head cheerleader.

"He certainly hasn't wasted any time," Amy said between her gritted teeth.

"Now, Amy—"

"Well, he hasn't!" Amy retorted hotly.

"What do you care?" Randi said. "You're the one who broke up with him, remember?"

Amy tossed her hair over her shoulder, her brown eyes flashing. "Well, he doesn't have to go out with every other girl in school two seconds later."

Randi folded her arms on the table. "What do you want him to do? Sit at home and pine for you? Wear a black veil?"

Amy couldn't help smiling. "You know what I mean."

"And just because they're sitting together doesn't necessarily mean anything," Randi pointed out. "You're jumping to conclusions. They're both on the student council, you know. Maybe—"

"Maybe they're having a student council meeting in the Annex during Thanksgiving break? Get serious."

"I think you should just ignore him. Unless you think you really like him after all," Randi added, studying her friend carefully.

"I don't like him," Amy insisted. "I mean, I like him as a friend, not as a boyfriend." The words caught in her throat. "Oh, no," she exclaimed in the next breath. "They're coming this way."

Amy snatched up her menu and pretended to study it closely as Rusty and Gwen passed by, but it was no use.

"Hi, Amy," Rusty mumbled. "Hey, Randi," he added.

To Randi's amazement Amy had turned beet red. "Hi, Gwen. Hi, Rusty," she said in a tiny voice, moving her eyes nervously back to the menu.

No one did anything for a long moment. Randi took in the scene, imagining what it would look like if someone took a picture: Amy with her eyes glued to the menu, Gwen and Rusty staring at her. It was an uncomfortable moment, but in an odd way, it reassured Randi. If these people—the coolest kids at school—could be tongue-tied, why couldn't she? The more she thought about it, the more reassured she felt.

Then Rusty struck his thumbs in his pockets and shrugged his shoulders. "W-well . . ." he stammered. "See you."

"See you," everyone else echoed. Then Rusty and Gwen left.

Amy pretended to study the menu for a

long time, not saying anything. Finally she looked up. "How embarrassing," she whispered.

Randi nodded sympathetically. "I still don't think he's going out with Gwen," she persisted.

"You really don't?" Amy asked. There seemed to be a twinge of hope in her voice.

"No. And I think you should make up your mind how you truly feel about him."

"I told you before—" Amy began.

"Think about it, okay?" Randi counseled.

Chapter Three

During the following week Randi spent hours making prints of the pictures she and Amy had taken in the park for the student photography contest. To her delight, her idea had been a good one: Most had turned out great. On Friday afternoon she gathered up the best ones to show Amy, then hurried to the gym for a meeting of the volunteers who were working on the Christmas dance.

The gymnasium was on the other side of the campus from the student darkroom, and she was in such a rush that at the gym door she almost crashed into a boy who was also on his way in. Randi's hand flew over her mouth when she saw who it was: Ned Taggert.

"Sorry," he apologized, stepping aside and fixing her with a deep, penetrating look.

Staring at the floor, Randi scurried past him, trying to stay cool. Still, she imagined his eyes were following her every move as she self-consciously headed for the bleachers.

To her relief, Amy was already there, but as Randi slid into the seat beside her, she got another shock. Sitting next to Amy was Gwen Davis, and the two of them were chatting away as though they were the closest of friends.

"Hi," Randi said breathlessly. She wondered if Ned was still looking at her.

Amy turned her head and smiled. "Hey, Rand. Nice outfit."

Randi flushed with pleasure. Her outfit—a stone-washed denim miniskirt, green pullover sweater, and matching green tights—was a little more daring than usual, and she was glad Amy liked it.

Amy's eyes fell to the envelope in Randi's hand. "What have you got? Pictures?" she asked excitedly.

"Uh-huh."

"From our day in the park?"

Randi nodded, handed her the envelope of pictures, and snuck a peek down the bleachers. Ned hadn't sat down yet. He was talking

29

with Miss Boone, the teacher in charge of the various dance committees. Normally formal and distant, Miss Boone seemed especially interested in what he was saying. Ned's charm, Randi realized, was hard to resist—even for teachers.

Beside her, Amy tore open the envelope of photographs and eagerly began examining them. "Horace Brockenborough's hands certainly came out good," she murmured. "Don't you think?" she added, politely tilting the picture toward Gwen.

"Mmmmm," Gwen agreed absently. Randi noticed that Gwen was sneaking little looks at Ned. Randi's eyes involuntarily followed hers. Ned had moved away from Miss Boone and was taking a seat at the foot of the bleachers, several rows below them.

Then Miss Boone called the meeting to order, and in a clipped, businesslike voice, announced that the theme of this year's dance was "A Christmas Fantasy."

"How original," Amy muttered under her breath, and Randi bit back a laugh.

"Let's get started," Miss Boone continued. "I'm going to read down the list of the various committees. Volunteers for each committee please raise your hands, and when I point to you, call out your last name." Pushing her glasses up on her nose, she looked down at the list in front of her. "All right, then. Volunteers to hang the decorations . . ."

Randi saw Ned's hand shoot up.

"What one do you want to volunteer for?" Amy whispered.

Randi shrugged. "How about making the crepe paper poinsettias?"

Amy nodded. "It sounds kind of boring, but okay. Is that okay with you?" she asked, turning to Gwen. Randi looked at her in surprise. Since when was Gwen suddenly included in their group?

"I think I'm going to volunteer to bake something," Gwen said nonchalantly. "Mother just hired the best new cook."

Randi thought that was cheating, but held her tongue. Then Miss Boone boomed, "Volunteers to make crepe paper flowers . . ."

Randi and Amy raised their hands, grinning at each other. But as Miss Boone pointed her pen and the other volunteers called out their last names, Randi felt herself tense up. A familiar, uneasy feeling came over her, her hands went clammy, and her pulse started to race. *This can't be happening,* she thought in despair. *I can't be nervous about calling out my own name.*

Then Miss Boone seemed to be pointing at her, and she nervously blurted out her name —at the same time that Amy called out hers.

"One at a time, please," Miss Boone said sternly. A couple of kids in the lower bleachers turned and stared in their direction.

Randi nudged Amy with her elbow, reddening, and Amy took the hint. "Bishop," she called out firmly.

There was a long pause. "Next! Next, please!" Miss Boone demanded. "We don't have all day."

Randi opened her mouth, but nothing came out. Her face felt like it was on fire. Then, to make matters worse, she noticed that Ned had turned his head and was looking up at her.

"H-H-Hinton," she stammered. There were a couple of snickers in the crowd. She wanted to crawl under the bleachers and hide.

After Miss Boone scribbled down her name, Ned turned around and faced the front again, and Randi tried to relax. At least he hadn't smiled when she stuttered. Instead, he seemed to be giving her that same, searching look.

Gwen hadn't missed a thing. "What's going on between you and Ned Taggert?" she whispered, leaning over. "He was really staring at you."

Amy nodded her head emphatically. "It's true, Randi," she said, sounding almost surprised.

Randi managed to collect herself. "Come on, you guys," she protested weakly. "He doesn't even know I exist."

Amy and Gwen seemed skeptical, but they dropped the subject. Could it be possible? Randi wondered. No way, she said to herself firmly. Ned probably thinks I'm a bumbling idiot.

After Miss Boone had compiled her list of the volunteers, the meeting broke up into the separate committees, and Gwen wandered off with the refreshments group, leaving Amy and Randi alone.

"What was that all about?" Randi asked immediately.

"What?"

"You and Gwen. I didn't know you two were such pals."

Amy blushed faintly. "I like Gwen."

"I like Gwen, too," Randi interjected. "But that's not what I meant. You're trying to find out if there's anything going on between her and Rusty, aren't you?"

"Do you think it was too obvious?" Amy asked guiltily.

"Not really." Randi smiled in spite of herself. "What did you find out?"

"Well," Amy said, then took a deep breath, "she's not going out with him."

"See!" Randi said triumphantly. "I told you."

"Not that I care who Rusty goes out with," Amy quickly added.

"And I'm the queen of England," Randi shot back.

"I don't want to talk about it," Amy mumbled. "Besides, I think what's going on with you and Ned is way more interesting."

"There's *nothing* going on between us," Randi insisted. But she had to admit, it would be kind of fun if there were.

"Did you get your photographs in on time?" Randi said into the phone two days later. The phone was wedged between her shoulder and ear as Randi tried to paint her toenails and talk to Amy at the same time. "Hold on a minute," she said, then maneuvered the phone into a more comfortable position. "There, that's better."

"I submitted them this morning," Amy said. The student photography exhibition and contest was set for the following week. "What are you going to wear to the reception?" she added. "Are you going to get dressed up?"

"Not really," Randi said. "The reception is right after last bell. I'd feel like a jerk being all dressed up for the entire day at school."

"Me, too." There was a long pause, and then Amy said dramatically, "I heard a rumor."

Randi's hand froze in midstroke. There was something in Amy's voice that suggested this was important gossip. "What?" she asked.

"I heard Ned likes you," Amy said flatly.

Randi didn't say anything at first, but a shiver of pleasure ran up her spine. "Really?" she said as casually as possible. She tried to continue painting her toes, but she had to stop. All of a sudden, she couldn't keep her hand steady.

"That's what Gwen heard," Amy said. "I think she's jealous," Amy added, almost sounding a little jealous herself.

"Gwen probably made it up."

"Why would she do that?"

"I don't know," Randi admitted. "Who did she hear it from?"

"Jimmy Vardy. And Jimmy and Ned are *best* friends."

Randi considered this, still not daring to think that what Amy had said was true. "That doesn't mean anything. I heard a rumor that he likes you." That wasn't true, but the words just tumbled out. Randi suddenly wanted to include Amy. She also wanted time to decide how she felt about Ned liking her. She wasn't ready for anybody like Ned.

"Really?" Amy sounded excited. "From who?"

Randi's heart sank. She should just admit the truth—right now. But that would be mean—Amy's voice sounded so full of hope. "Umm, Brenda Chen," she replied after a minute.

"How does she know?" Amy demanded.

"I don't know," Randi mumbled.

"I wish he did." Amy sighed, then added. "You're not interested in him, are you?"

"No, I told you already," Randi said automatically. She made herself remember the way he'd smirked at her in English class, but that image seemed to have faded from her brain, and only his deep blue-gray eyes remained. "I don't like him," she lied. *I could never get him anyway,* she thought, *so what's the point?*

"Well, I do," Amy said. "I hope Brenda Chen is right."

Amy's teasing about her and Ned kept him firmly in the front of Randi's mind for the next few days, no matter how hard she tried not to think about him. *Ned could have anyone he wanted*, she told herself. *He can't really be interested in me.*

One afternoon after school she was sitting at the kitchen table, an empty yellow pad and half a dozen sharpened pencils in front of her, trying to decide on a subject for her class speech. She couldn't seem to think of a thing. Instead of notes, the pad was covered with the word *Ned*, doodled over and over. With a sigh, she crumpled up the sheet of paper and tossed it into the wastebasket under the sink. What was wrong with her? She couldn't be falling in love with him, could she? That would be totally ridiculous. She didn't even know him.

Her thoughts were interrupted as her mother arrived home from work. "Hi, honey," her mother called. Mrs. Hinton seemed in a particularly good mood that day.

"Hi, Mom," Randi said listlessly.

"Something the matter?" she asked. "That wasn't a very enthusiastic 'Hi, Mom.' "

"I'm having trouble deciding on a topic for my class speech, that's all," Randi said. She couldn't bring herself to admit that she was daydreaming about a boy she hardly knew.

"Maybe I can help you," Mrs. Hinton suggested, sitting down next to her.

"It's no use," Randi sighed. "I've been racking my brain all afternoon, and I haven't come up with a single idea."

"Well, what have some of the other students spoken about?"

Randi knit her brow. "All kinds of things. Their hobbies, trips they took, sports . . ."

"What about the trip we took to the Grand Canyon last summer?" Mrs. Hinton suggested. They had gone to visit Randi's Uncle David, who lived in nearby Flagstaff. "I thought that was very interesting."

Randi had to admit it wasn't a bad idea. She had saved all her souvenirs, so she did have some material for research. Then all at once, a mental picture of her standing in front of the entire student body flashed through her mind, and she shuddered involuntarily.

"Honey?" her mother said softly, leaning across the table. "What is it?"

Randi sighed. "I never told you this before," she began reluctantly, "but the thought of giving this speech is making me so nervous . . ."

"You have stage fright?" her mother asked. She nodded her head in understanding. "I wonder if it's hereditary. I used to hate to speak in front of people too."

"You did?" Randi was amazed. She had seen her mother give several speeches before for her work with the community board, and she was always cool and relaxed-looking.

"When I was growing up, I used to stutter and turn red and have heart palpitations," her mother admitted. "It embarrassed me terribly."

"How did you get over it, Mom?"

"I just gritted my teeth and did it. And after a couple of times I realized that standing up in front of a group of people wasn't all that bad. The world didn't collapse if I made a mistake, and in fact, nobody really seemed to be paying that much attention to my mistakes anyway. You know," she added softly, "sometimes we think other people are more interested in us than they really are." She looked at Randi levelly. "It's silly to be that self-conscious."

With a sinking feeling Randi thought of Ned. Was he interested, or was that all a figment of her imagination? Had he really noticed her at all?

"Now, sweetheart, don't worry about it," her mother continued, misinterpreting her daughter's silence. "And in the meantime I have something that might make you feel better," she added, sounding pleased with herself. With that, she disappeared into the dining room and a moment later, reappeared carrying a large, powder blue dress box that said La Vogue across the top. Randi gulped. La Vogue was one of the most fashionable shops in town.

"W-what is it?" she asked.

"An early Christmas present!" Her mother smiled, placing the box on the kitchen table.

"Are you sure we can afford it?" Randi asked uncertainly.

"Don't worry about it, sweetheart," her mother assured her. "You deserve a new dress for the Christmas dance, and you're going to have one. We can't afford to buy *a lot* of new clothes, but I can't see why you shouldn't have something nice for a special occasion. And the Christmas dance is a special occasion." Her mother paused, looking at Randi expectantly. "Go ahead, open it."

Randi removed the lid of the box and pushed aside the mauve tissue paper lining on the inside. "Oh, Mom," she gasped, gingerly lifting the dress out.

It was made from yards of deep blue taffeta and looked very grown up, with an off-the-shoulder neckline and a flared skirt. "I love it," Randi said immediately, holding it up in front of her. She gave her mom a huge hug.

"I've giving it to you now so that we can see if it needs any alterations," her mother said. "Run upstairs and try it on. Go ahead."

Randi was off in a flash. *I've got the perfect dress for the dance*, Randi thought. *Now all I need is the perfect date.*

Chapter Four

The reception for the student photography exhibition was in Tunstall Lounge, a large, oak-paneled study room that was named for one of Brockenborough Prep's chief philanthropists, Mrs. Libby Tunstall. Appropriately the first person Randi spotted when she arrived was Mrs. Tunstall herself, who looked very elegant with her sleek hairdo and off-white wool suit, accented with several large pieces of gold jewelry. She was talking to one of the students and gesturing with her hand, her expensive bracelets jangling noisily.

Randi's gaze moved to the photographs lining the room. Each one had been mounted in a clear Plexiglas frame, and they looked very striking hanging against the oak walls. She spotted her photo of Horace Brockenborough's hands near the far corner. A knot of people were clustered around it, and Randi felt a tiny surge of pride.

Amy was nowhere in sight. Feeling suddenly unsure of herself, Randi hovered near the door for a moment, then edged toward the punch bowl that had been set up on a long mahogany desk in the center of the lounge. Having something to do with her hands, she decided, would make her feel more comfortable. The thought of her class speech suddenly pushed its way into her mind, but she forced herself to ignore it as she reached for a glass.

Randi felt herself relaxing after a glass of the fruity, refreshing punch. Randi wandered over to the photograph hanging nearest the punch bowl—a tight close-up of a Siamese cat's face—and tried to look casual. After studying the picture carefully and deciding she liked it, her eyes timidly swept the room, lingering on the three teachers who were judging the exhibit. They were making notes in front of one of the other photographs. Randi forced herself to look away. It would be nice to win one of the ribbons, Randi thought, but she didn't think she had a chance.

Just then Amy appeared at the door and came right over to her. "Where have you been all day?" she demanded. "Where were you at third bell?" It was their routine to meet in the girl's room every day at that time because their lunch schedules only coincided twice a week.

"I had to stay behind in algebra because I didn't understand one of the problems from last week's quiz," Randi explained. "What's up?"

Amy had the strangest look on her face. "You'll never guess what happened!" she whispered. "I—"

Randi noticed that Mrs. Tunstall was gliding over to them and put her finger to her lips.

"Hello, girls!" Mrs. Tunstall trilled.

Randi and Amy murmured polite hellos.

"Such a lovely reception, isn't it?" Mrs. Tunstall said, not waiting for an answer. "The students are so *gifted* here at Brockenborough. Which of these pictures is yours, my dear?" Mrs. Tunstall asked Randi.

Randi pointed shyly across the room, then wondered if it had been rude to point. "The one of the statue's hands . . ." She felt nervous, but at least she wasn't stuttering.

"Oh, yes," Mrs. Tunstall broke in enthusiastically. "It's one of my favorites." Her face broke into a wide smile. "I'm sure the judges will agree with me," she added, patting Randi's shoulder lightly. "What is your name again, dear?"

Randi felt the faintest ripple of self-confidence wash over her. "Randi Hinton, ma'am. And thank you."

Mrs. Tunstall turned to Amy politely. "And which one is yours, Amy?"

Amy gestured toward the print she had selected. It showed a statue of the Greek god Mercury poised dramatically against the winter sky.

"That's a very good one, too," Mrs. Tunstall cooed. "My, there is so much talent in this school." She drew herself up and patted her hair. "But that's to be expected from Brockenborough students, I suppose. Well, girls, it was lovely talking to you," she said in the next breath, and after a tiny wave, she glided away.

"What a character," Amy said fondly.

"She's very sweet," Randi agreed, still warmed by Mrs. Tunstall's compliment. *Wouldn't it be amazing if I did win a ribbon*, she thought. She had never really hoped to win.

Amy jolted her back to reality, grabbing her by the arm. "I *have* to tell you what happened!" she said, arching her eyebrows meaningfully.

Randi forced herself to forget about the judging and concentrate on her friend's news. "Over here," she said, drawing Amy over to a couch opposite the punch bowl.

Amy sat down, looking like she was about to burst. "I had a long conversation with *him* today," she said, her eyes flashing.

All at once Randi didn't feel so buoyant. "Him?" she asked, although she already knew exactly who Amy was talking about.

"Ned," Amy said dreamily. "He is so adorable."

"What did you talk about?"

"Actually we didn't talk that long," Amy admitted. "But we talked about the dance for a while." She paused dramatically. "And he doesn't have a date."

"Did he ask you?" Randi blurted out. It was the first thing that had popped into her mind, and now she wished she could take it back. It sounded so petty.

But her remark didn't seem to faze Amy at all. "He didn't ask me," she replied, "but I'm working on it," she added, biting her lip mischievously.

"What about Rusty?" Randi asked in an accusing tone. *Rusty really likes her,* Randi thought with irritation. *Why doesn't she leave*

46

Ned alone? Amy shot her a look, and Randi let the subject drop. "Let's go check out the other photographs," she suggested instead.

But the idea of Ned taking Amy to the Christmas dance stayed with Randi like a dark, depressing cloud hovering over the reception room. At the same time she felt guilty. After all, Amy *was* her best friend, and Randi wanted her to be happy. Besides, in all fairness, she had told Amy she didn't like Ned. Randi shook her head. She still felt miserable. She tried to rationalize. *Amy has a better chance with him than I do*, she thought. Why would he be interested in plain old Randi Hinton? But if he wasn't interested, a little voice inside her argued, why did he keep giving her those penetrating looks? And why couldn't she get him out of her mind?

Just before the reception ended, Mr. Massey, Brockenborough Prep's headmaster, made a short speech: "First of all, I'd like to congratulate all the exhibitors," he began, casually running his hand through his silver hair. "This is a fine body of work. I'd also like to thank Mrs. Tunstall for sponsoring this event."

There was polite applause for Mrs. Tunstall, who beamed with pleasure, but Randi's mind was concentrated on the speaker. The headmaster seemed so relaxed speaking in front of the crowd, she thought, so confident. What was his secret?

"The judges' ribbons will be posted first thing tomorrow morning," Mr. Massey concluded. "Again, thank you for coming, and thank you, Mrs. Tunstall."

Randi joined in the applause, still trying to analyze Mr. Massey's speaking style. He seemed to be talking to everyone individually, even though he was addressing a crowd. How did he do it? she wondered.

"Earth calling Randi," Amy murmured, giving her a sly poke in the ribs. "What are you thinking about? You have the funniest look on your face."

"I was thinking about my class speech," Randi sighed ruefully.

"Have you decided on a topic yet?" Amy asked.

"Well, I was thinking about doing it on our trip to the Grand Canyon last summer," Randi said, looking for Amy's reaction.

"That sounds pretty good," Amy said, not sounding that interested at all.

"Do you *really* think so?"

"Go for it," Amy said, and shrugged.

The next morning was overcast, the damp promise of snow lingering in the air. Randi loved this kind of weather, and she decided to walk to school. As she strolled briskly down Hewitt Drive, her thought returned to the photography reception the afternoon before. She had been so caught up in what Amy had said about Ned that she hadn't thought much about the event itself. Or the contest. With a start she realized that the ribbons were probably up by now. She decided to stop by the lounge before classes and see who won.

Then she paused. What if she ran into somebody she knew? It could be embarrassing, especially if she hadn't won. Still, she was dying to know. She remembered that the lounge was mainly used in the afternoon, although a few students occasionally studied there in the morning. *Probably no one would be there so early,* she reasoned. She decided to take a chance and dart in.

When she was two blocks from the pair of stone lions that flanked Brockenborough Prep's entrance, it began to snow. Thick flakes frosted her eyelashes as Randi lifted her face up to the swirling snow. She slowed her pace, shivering with delight. She loved snow. Wishing she could linger outside a little longer, she reluctantly hurried up the steps to Monroe Hall.

Inside, the hallway was deserted. She smiled

49

to herself. She had panicked for nothing. There wouldn't be anyone in the lounge. Feeling bold, she quickly slipped down the corridor and went through the door marked "Tunstall."

She quickly peeled off her gloves, which were damp with the melting snow. Then all at once she realized she wasn't alone. In the corner a boy was studying one of the photographs, his back to her. With a jolt Randi realized he was looking at her picture of the statue's hands. She was about to slip out of the room when he turned suddenly.

"Hello," he said pleasantly. *It was Ned Taggert!*

"Hi." Randi froze and looked down at the Persian carpet on the floor. She felt like a total fool for stopping there so early.

"Is it snowing out?" Ned asked.

She looked up at him timidly. Once again, his deep blue eyes seemed to be boring right into her.

"Uh-huh," she managed to say, wondering what her hair looked like. Shaking her head and feeling self-conscious, she flipped a blonde curl behind one ear as casually as possible.

"I love it when it snows," he said.

"Me too," Randi replied, dropping one of her gloves. She felt like a total klutz.

In a flash Ned bent over and retrieved it. As he handed it to her, their hands brushed together, and Ned smiled at her. That same penetrating look remained in his eyes.

"You're Randi Hinton, right?" he asked quietly.

She couldn't believe that he knew her name. "Uh-huh," she said, forcing a shy smile. "And you're Ned Taggert."

"Yup," he said. "I guess we sort of know each other even though we've never met."

Randi's heart started to thump.

"Randi . . ." Ned said slowly, as if running the name over in his mind. "Is that short for something?"

"No, it's just Randi," she said, noticing how long and thick his eyelashes were. "My father wanted a boy," she added, grinning.

Ned smiled back, and there was a long pause. "By the way, congratulations," he said suddenly. Randi stared at him, puzzled. "For your ribbon," Ned explained. Standing aside, he pointed at the red ribbon stuck on the wall next to her photograph. She had won second prize.

"Oh!" Randi flushed and a feeling of pride washed over her. "I really didn't expect that," she said modestly, already feeling less unsure of herself.

"I think you should have gotten first prize," Ned said, pointing to the blue-ribbon winner, the close-up of the Siamese cat. "I mean, it's okay and all," he allowed, "but I think yours is much more interesting."

To her surprise, Randi felt the last trace of her nervousness fall away. Ned was so natural, so matter-of-fact, that it seemed to be catching. "Are you interested in photography?" she asked, surprised at how easily the question came out.

"Only as a spectator. I'm not any good at it myself." Ned ran his fingers through his thick, sandy hair.

"It's not that hard," Randi said. "If *I* can do it—"

"Sure *you* can, that's the point," he said. "You have a talent for it."

Just then the first bell sounded, and Randi's spirits sank. If only they could talk a little longer, she thought, especially now that she felt so under control. Reluctantly she edged toward the door. Ned tipped his head to one side, looking surprised. "Aren't you going to study here this period?" he asked.

"Um, no," Randi admitted.

"Oh," Ned replied, sounding disappointed. "Well, congratulations again. Maybe I'll see you around."

Randi felt her face getting warm. "Thanks." She walked to the door and paused, wishing she wasn't such a coward.

"Maybe you could give me a lesson sometime," Ned called.

She turned her head. He was looking at her again in the same, intense way, she saw with a thrill. His eyes were so blue. "A lesson?"

"In photography."

"Oh, um, sure." She gulped. When Ned didn't reply, she stood there uncomfortably for a long moment, then murmured, "See you," again and slipped out the door.

Out in the hall, she grimaced and shook her head. That was her big chance, and she'd handled it all wrong, she thought dejectedly. Ned must think she was some kind of idiot. Why hadn't she set up a photo lesson right then and there? she thought. But maybe that would seem too forward. *Why am I so confused?* she wondered. Because you're falling in love, said a tiny voice deep inside her.

Chapter Five

Two days later Amy and Randi were meeting for their usual chat in the girl's room during the break between third and fourth period. As Amy brushed her hair, she turned the conversation to a subject that Randi was trying to forget.

"So, how's your speech coming?" she said.

"Okay, I guess," Randi answered, sensing a strange note in her friend's voice. "Why?"

"Well, I had an idea. Something that might help you."

Randi looked at her doubtfully. "And what is that?" Amy put her brush away and began rummaging through her purse. "Hiring someone to impersonate me?"

"Very funny," Amy said dryly. "Want some lip gloss?" she asked, holding out the tube.

Randi shook her head. "Seriously, do you have a suggestion? This is no joke to me, you know."

"I know it isn't." Amy sounded sincere. "I'm really trying to help. I thought we could go to hear the debate team this afternoon. They're debating Madison High at four o'clock."

"Amy, I don't want to become a member of the debate team. All I want to do is get through my class speech." Randi looked at her friend suspiciously. "Since when are you so interested in debating anyway?"

"Well, it *is* public speaking, which is your problem," Amy began, starting to wither under Randi's steely gaze. "Okay, okay." She grinned, shrugging her shoulders. "I might as well tell you. There is one other reason: the captain of the debate team."

"Ned Taggert," Randi said softly.

"Well, I told you about that long conversation we had last week," Amy said defensively.

"I remember," Randi said, thinking of her own conversation with Ned in Tunstall Lounge. Somehow she hadn't gotten around to telling Amy about it. Now certainly didn't seem like the right time.

"So, do you want to go? I'm too chicken to go by myself," Amy admitted in a whisper.

"Do I have to?" The idea of watching Amy flirt with Ned wasn't very appealing.

"*Randi*! It'll help you with your speech. You're bound to pick up some pointers. Come on, please."

"Well . . ." Randi paused, unsure. Deep down she wanted to see Ned again. She wanted to see if he looked at her with the same intense expression in his eyes.

"Great, it's settled," Amy said firmly, tossing her lip gloss into her purse. "I'll meet you in front of the auditorium at three forty-five."

"Oh, all right," Randi said dubiously.

After her friend had left, Randi studied her outfit in the mirror and frowned. The pair of baggy green corduroy overalls and the navy top she had put on that morning were comfortable, but they didn't look that terrific. Had she known she was going to see Ned that day, she would have worn something a little more flattering.

The two teams of debaters were already onstage, sitting in black folding chairs, as Amy led Randi down the center aisle of Kearney Auditorium. Randi studied them out of the corner of her eye. Sure enough Ned was there, sitting right in the middle of the front row. Since he was under a spotlight that shaded his eyes, it was difficult to tell what he was looking at, but Randi had the distinct impression he had noticed them come in. She fastened her gaze to the back of Amy's head and tried to be nonchalant.

Suddenly she realized how far down the aisle they had gone. Where was Amy planning to sit, anyway? Randi wondered. In Ned's lap? "Amy!" she hissed in a low voice.

Amy turned her head with a dramatic flip of her hair.

"Not so far down," Randi whispered.

"Well, where do you want to sit?"

Randi imagined that everyone in the auditorium was staring at them. "How about right here?" she asked, pointing at two empty seats in the third row.

"Fine with me," Amy said with a shrug.

As they arranged themselves in their seats, Randi realized with a sinking feeling how close they were to the stage. They were practically on top of the podium, and she wished Amy had been a little more subtle about choosing their seats. Evidently Amy felt the same way. First she fussed with her knapsack, wedging it under the seat. Then she busied herself searching through her purse, all the time avoiding looking up, as if she didn't want to look Ned in the eye. Finally she leaned over to whisper in Randi's ear, "Is he looking at me?"

Randi casually glanced at the stage. It was hard to tell where Ned was looking, but it seemed to be in their direction. "I can't really tell," she replied.

Amy followed her glance, just as casually. At that moment Ned turned his head away and murmured something to the boy sitting behind him. Amy sighed and frowned.

Then Mr. Harvey, the debate team's advisor, called the assembly to order. "Today, we'd like to welcome Madison High to Brockenborough," he began. "The two teams will be debating the merits of the American jury system. As the result of a coin toss earlier, Brockenborough will be debating in favor of trial by jury, and Madison, against." Mr. Harvey paused, then sneezed loudly into his handkerchief. "All right, speakers," he continued without missing a beat. "Today's topic: 'Is justice best served by a jury of one's peers?' "

"Snoresville," Amy muttered in Randi's ear.

She settled back into her seat as if she were about to take a nap.

"Brockenborough will begin," Mr. Harvey continued. "Mr. Taggert?"

When Ned stood up and walked to the podium, Amy straightened up and looked at the stage attentively. Randi, on the other hand, shrank back into her seat, embarrassed to be sitting so close.

Ned cleared his throat and pulled his notes out of his blazer pocket. After a short pause he took a deep breath and said in a clear voice. "There can be no valid argument made against our present judicial system." He waited a moment to let this sink in, and as he scanned the audience, his eyes locked on the two girls in the third row.

Amy prodded Randi with her elbow.

"My opponents might argue that jury selection is left to chance . . ." Ned continued, still staring in their direction. It seemed as though he had forgotten everyone else in the room.

Randi didn't hear a word he said, but was hypnotized by his eyes as a thrilling sensation flooded over her. He was looking at her, she knew it. Amy poked her again a little harder, and the thrill subsided. Amy obviously thought he was looking at *her*. Randi hesitated, confused. Could it be possible? she wondered, feeling betrayed. Exactly who *was* he looking at, anyway?

Randi relaxed when he focused his glance on another row. She could now concentrate on other things—his blue blazer and bright yellow tie, the way his sandy hair curled over his ears, the habit he had of gesturing with his index finger. She tried to pay attention to what he was saying, but she had a hard time concentrating.

Mr. Harvey called time on Ned before he reached his conclusion, and he sat down, looking frustrated. Randi forced her eyes away from him and tried to listen to the next debater. For the rest of the debate she studied the speakers' techniques for hints on delivering her own speech. The one thing they all seemed to project was self-confidence, she realized, her heart sinking. *How do you get that kind of self-confidence?* she wondered.

Before she knew it, the debate had ended, and the judges declared Brockenborough's team the winner. Amy leaned over to whisper in her ear. "Was it just my imagination?" she asked, sounding like she was about to burst, "or was he really staring at me when I nudged you?"

Randi didn't have the heart to tell her what she really thought. "He was definitely looking over here," she said vaguely. Out of the corner of her eye she saw Ned leaving the stage. "I think we'd better talk about this later," she added in a half-whisper, shooting Amy a significant look.

No sooner had she said this than Ned suddenly appeared at their side. There was no question about who he was looking at now. "Hi, Randi," he said, staring at her intently.

"Hi," Randi replied softly. Amy seemed to turn to stone beside her.

"I've never seen you at any of our debates before," Ned went on, then paused. "Hi, Amy," he added.

"Hey, Ned," Amy said flatly, sounding plainly disappointed.

There was a very long, drawn-out pause, then Amy took Ned's hint and picked up her knapsack. "I've got to get going," she said reluctantly. "I've got some stuff to do for my mother."

"See you," Ned said gratefully, as if he'd been waiting to talk to Randi alone.

"I'll call you," Amy told Randi, holding her eyes for a long moment. It was hard to tell what she was thinking. Then, with a half-smile and a wave, she was gone.

Randi tried to stay calm. She knew Amy well enough to know when she was truly upset, and even though she didn't look exactly thrilled, she seemed okay. Now if Randi could only keep herself under control in front of Ned. Now that they were alone, it seemed so much harder.

"So . . ." Ned said at last. "Are you thinking of trying out for the team? We can always use fresh debaters."

"*Me*?" Randi exclaimed, before she could catch herself. She bit back a rueful smile. "No, I would be the world's worst debater. I can't stand speaking in public," she admitted. "Actually I came hoping to pick up some pointers. For my class speech."

"Maybe I could give you some tips," he said shyly. His eyes suddenly moved to hers, and the expression in them nearly made her melt inside.

"All right," she said softly.

"As a trade, though," he added, his eyes twinkling mischievously.

"A trade for what?"

"You have to give me photography lessons."

Randi flushed with pride. At least he wasn't making her feel like a complete dope. "It's a deal," she said, nodding her head.

"Great." Ned flashed her a brilliant smile. "When's your class speech?"

"January tenth."

"We'd better get together pretty soon, then," he said. "With the holidays and all, there isn't a lot of time. What's your topic?"

"My trip last summer to the Grand Canyon."

Ned didn't seem to react to her topic one way or the other. "When's a good time for you?" he asked instead.

She shrugged. Her schedule wasn't that busy, but she didn't want him to think she was *too* available. "Wednesday afternoons are usually pretty good for me," she said shyly.

"Hmmm." He frowned. "That's not good for me. I have yearbook committee meetings on Wednesdays."

"How about Tuesday afternoon?"

"I coach peewee-league basketball on Tuesdays."

Randi forced herself to smile. "Maybe you should tell *me* when a good time for you is."

Ned scratched the back of his head. "Well, actually the best time for me would be at night." He looked down at the floor. "Actually what I really would like to do is take you out."

Randi could hardly believe her ears. A wave

of astonishment flooded over her. "Th-that would be nice," she stammered.

"Good," he said quietly, with a bashful smile. A look of relief seemed to come over his face. "How about Friday night? Maybe I could coach you a little first, and then we could go out for something to eat afterward. Sort of half-work, half-date."

"Sounds great," Randi said, recovering her poise.

"I'll call you Thursday, then," he said, and after a final piercing look, he took off. Randi stood there numbly for a moment, then joined the crowd shuffling out of the auditorium. The idea of dating Ned, she realized, was going to take some getting used to.

She and Amy had planned to start making crepe paper flowers that night for the Christmas dance, and the thought of it filled Randi with dread. How was Amy going to react when she heard that Ned had asked her out? It made her feel guilty, as if she were sneaking around behind her best friend's back.

To her relief, Amy seemed calm enough when she greeted her at the door. "Now don't be shocked," Amy said lightly as they headed up the enormous carved oak staircase that led to her bedroom on the second floor.

"There's a ton of crepe paper. We're going to have to make a lot of poinsettias."

Amy wasn't kidding. As soon as Randi saw the bundles of crepe paper neatly stacked on the floor, her mouth fell open. "This is going to take years!"

"I know." Amy shook her head glumly. "The other two volunteers dropped out, so Miss Boone gave me the extra material and asked if we could make as many flowers as possible."

"All right." Randi pulled off her coat with a sigh. "Do you have the pipe cleaners and the streamers?"

Amy gestured to three enormous cartons next to her bed. "And the glitter and the stems and the rubber bands and the wire. Have you ever made these before?" Randi shook her head. "It's very simple," Amy said. "First you fold the crepe paper into quarters like this," she demonstrated, her fingers flying. "Then you twist it in the center, fluff it out, and anchor it with a pipe cleaner. Okay? It's pretty easy."

Randi watched her dubiously. "I guess."

"Here," Amy said, thrusting a stack of crepe paper in front of her. "You fold, and I'll do the pipe cleaners."

This assembly line approach seemed to

work, and after a few false starts, they began turning out perfect flowers.

"So . . ." Amy cleared her throat meaningfully, breaking the silence. "I guess you have a few things to tell me." She shot Randi a faintly accusatory look.

Randi froze in midflower. She had been rehearsing what she was going to say to Amy, but her mind had suddenly gone blank.

"I'm really sorry," she finally managed. "I hope you didn't think I was sneaking around behind your back. I ran into him a couple of days before in the lounge and we just started talking."

"Well, he was really giving you the eye!" Amy exclaimed. "At first I felt a little jealous, but I'm really glad for you. Did he ask you out?" she added casually.

"Uh-huh," Randi said. This was turning out to be much easier than she thought it would be.

"He did?" Amy sounded surprised. "Boy, Rand, I have to hand it to you. Half the girls in school would give anything to be in your shoes."

"You really don't mind?" Randi asked in a tiny voice.

Amy reached over and gave her friend's shoulder a quick squeeze. "I think it's really great that he likes you. Really. When are you going out, anyway?"

"Friday night." Randi's eyes sparkled with excitement. "Now all we have to do is get you and Rusty back together again, and everything will be perfect," she blurted out.

Amy looked at her with curiosity. "You keep pushing Rusty so much, I'm beginning to wonder. I mean, what's so great about Rusty?"

"That's exactly what I want you to find out," Randi answered. "He's crazy about you. You just need to give him a second chance."

Chapter Six

"Ouch!" Randi grimaced. "*Mom!*"

"Sorry, darling," her mother murmured, her words muffled by the straight pins clenched between her teeth. "Did I stick you?"

"A little." Randi sighed, realizing how rude she had sounded. She was on edge, though. It was Thursday night, and she was expecting a phone call from Ned any minute to make plans for their date.

"I'll try to be more careful." Her mother stood back to look at Randi, who was posed on the kitchen stepstool, her arms held awkwardly out to the side. They were working on the alterations to the bodice of her new dress for the Christmas dance. "I think it looks

68

better now," Mrs. Hinton said with a satisfied air. She glanced at her watch. "I'm afraid that's all I have time for now, honey. Charles is due any minute. We'll work on the hemline tomorrow, okay?"

"I didn't know Charles was coming over," Randi said. "Are you going out?"

"Didn't I tell you?" her mother murmured, rapidly repacking her sewing box. "We're going to the community board meeting at Assembly Hall." This wasn't very surprising to Randi. Both Charles and her mother were very active in local politics. That was how they had met in the first place.

"Maybe you did, but I can't remember," Randi replied. It was just as well, she thought. It would be much easier to talk to Ned on the phone if there wasn't anyone at home to overhear her.

Mrs. Hinton handed her a quilted hanger. "Hang the dress on my closet door, will you? Maybe I'll get a chance to work on it tonight after I get home," she said.

"Okay, Mom. But if you're too tired, it can wait until tomorrow."

Charles arrived while Randi was in her bedroom taking off the dress. Straining her ears, she heard him greet her mother, and then there was a short silence. Randi imagined that they were kissing. It felt weird to imagine her mother kissing anyone, and she quickly put it out of her mind. There were more important things to think about. Like Ned's phone call. Quickly changing back into jeans and a sweater, she went out to say hello to Charles. Her main purpose was to hurry them out of the house as quickly as possible so that she could have some privacy when the phone rang.

Breezing into the kitchen, she found her mother standing at the sink. Charles was standing opposite her. "Hi, Charles," Randi said.

"How's my favorite girl?" he replied gallantly.

Randi colored slightly. His compliments always made her feel self-conscious. "F-fine," she stammered, cursing herself.

"Good, good," Charles boomed. Tonight he was wearing a pale pink shirt that looked nice with his complexion, which was ruddy from the cold weather. "I hear you two have been working on a new dress for the Christmas dance."

"Uh-huh." Randi nodded, then froze as the telephone rang.

Her mother picked it up casually. "Hello?" she said. "Yes, she's here," she added after a moment. "Who's calling, please?" With a slight raising of her eyebrows, she handed the phone toward Randi. "Ned Taggert," she said.

"Umm, I'll take it in your bedroom." Randi blushed, then darted out of the kitchen, her heart pounding.

She picked up the phone gingerly a moment later. "I've got it, Mom," she said in the most normal voice she could muster. There was a click on the other end as her mother hung up. "Hello?"

"Hi there," he said. He even *sounded* handsome, she decided.

"Hi." A pause.

"So, are we still on for tomorrow night?" His voice was confident and strong in comparison to how Randi imagined she sounded.

"Um, sure."

"Do you have anything particular you want to do?"

Her mind was a total blank. "Um, no."

"Well . . ." he exhaled loudly. "I thought maybe we could go to Shakey's for a pizza."

"That sounds fine," Randi wished she could think of something funny or clever to say, but all she could seem to concentrate on was not stammering.

"About the speech lesson I promised you," he went on. "I can't really think of a place to practice on a Friday night, can you?"

Randi paused. The coaching he had promised her was the last thing she had been thinking about. "Not really," she answered.

"Well, I was wondering," he said uneasily, "do you mind if we sort of postpone it for another time? I can't stay out too late tomorrow anyway because I've got a basketball scrimmage in Brattleboro Saturday morning."

"I don't mind at all," Randi said honestly. In a way it was a relief. She didn't want to spend their whole first date talking about schoolwork. She wanted to get to know him first.

"I could give you some pointers on the way over to Shakey's if you want," he added.

"That would be great."

"Okay. Pick you up at seven-thirty?"

"Great."

After she hung up, Randi headed straight for her closet. She had to find something to wear tomorrow night. As she was critically examining a row of blouses, there was a knock at the door and her mother's head popped into view. "We're going out now," she announced, then paused expectantly. "Everything okay?"

Randi realized that her mother was subtly asking what the phone call had been all about. "Everything's fine," she said, realizing that her excitement was written all over her face. "I'm, ah, going out tomorrow night with Ned," she added, biting back a smile.

"That's nice, dear. I'll be back around ten-thirty," her mother went on, as if going out with Ned Taggert was an everyday occurrence. Blowing Randi a kiss, she closed the door behind her. Randi went back to her closet, madly throwing together possible outfits. Tomorrow night had to be perfect.

The next day seemed to drag on forever, and Randi checked her watch constantly, calculating how much longer it would be until seven-thirty.

After chemistry lab, she went to the cafeteria for lunch, where she ran into Brenda Chen. They had just set their trays down at a table full of cheerleaders when Randi spotted Ned out of the corner of her eye. He was on his way out, talking to his friend Craig Ambler. Randi wasn't sure what to do, but she didn't want to stare, so she reached for the pepper and began shaking it on her tuna salad.

Just as Ned passed their table, Vicki Greene, the head cheerleader, called out his name.

Ned paused, and to Randi's horror, Vicki started to flirt with him. How would Ned react? *Maybe he doesn't really like me,* Randi thought in a panic. Squaring her shoulders, she gathered her nerve and looked at him.

His eyes immediately locked with hers. "Hi, Randi," he said in a low, soft voice, completely ignoring what Vicki was saying.

"Hi," Randi murmured, turning bright red. She could see Vicki's mouth drop open out of the corner of her eye.

"Come on, Ned," Craig broke in. "We're going to be late."

Ned couldn't seem to move. "Okay," he said to Craig, waving him away. "See you at seven-thirty, Randi," he added, smiling at her. Then he was gone.

The lunch table seemed to freeze, and Randi could feel everyone looking at her. Trying to be as nonchalant as possible, she took a bite from her fruit cup and tried to think of something—anything—to say.

Vicki Greene broke the silence. "You have a *date* with Ned tonight?" Vicki sounded like it was the most unbelievable thing she had ever heard.

"Um, yeah," Randi said, taking a big gulp of milk.

"You do?" Brenda chimed in.

"Uh-huh," Randi replied, a little stung that even she sounded so amazed.

Yet as she finished her lunch, Randi felt

the mood of the table subtly change. Every now and then she caught one of the other girls staring at her, as if they were seeing her for the first time. There seemed to be a new look in her classmates' eyes, a look of respect, maybe even acceptance. Little by little, she was beginning to feel like she belonged.

Randi changed outfits four times that night before finally selecting a pair of baggy khaki pants and a soft red sweater. The doorbell rang promptly at seven-thirty, and as arranged, her mother answered it. Randi forced herself to count to twenty-five before she took her coat and went into the foyer.

"You won't be out too late, will you, Ned?" her mother was saying as she entered. Randi cringed. She hoped her mother hadn't said anything embarrassing.

"No, ma'am, we won't," Ned replied. "We're just going to Shakey's for a bite to eat. And anyway, I have to get an eight o'clock bus tomorrow morning. We have a basketball scrimmage in Brattleboro."

Mrs. Hinton seemed pleased. "Good luck." Then she realized Randi was standing behind her. "Well, here she is," she said rather breathlessly.

Randi forced herself to smile. Her mother almost seemed more nervous than she was.

"Hi!" To her relief, she wasn't blushing and her heart wasn't pounding. Instead she was thinking about how nice Ned looked in his jeans and down jacket and how proud she felt being his date.

"Have a good time," her mother said, edging out of the foyer. "Nice to meet you, Ned."

"Nice to meet you, too, Mrs. Hinton." After helping Randi on with her coat, he opened the storm door behind him awkwardly. They walked out onto the porch. The night was still and bitingly cold, but Randi hardly noticed it. She was too excited—and too nervous.

Ned's car, a bright red MG convertible, was parked at the end of the driveway. The MG was a familiar sight around Brockenborough. No matter what the weather was like, he always seemed to be driving around with the top down, his sandy hair blowing in the breeze.

Tonight was no exception. "Do you mind if we leave the top down?" he asked as he opened the door for her and she slid in.

"No," Randi murmured, trying to sound nonchalant. It was freezing out!

"Great," Ned said, reaching into the backseat and pulling out a cozy-looking plaid wool throw. "Bundle up in this," he said. "It's awfully cold out tonight."

Randi clumsily draped the blanket around herself as Ned got into the driver's seat and started the car, revving the engine. "It takes a while for the heat to go on," he explained.

"The heat?" Randi asked. *With the top down*? she thought.

He seemed to read her mind. "You don't want us to freeze, do you?" he asked, a smile playing on his lips. "Wait a minute," he added, turning toward her. "Let me help you fix that," he said, tugging at the blanket.

As he helped arrange it around her shoulders, his hand brushed against her cheek accidentally, sending an electric thrill down her back. Randi's cheek was still tingling as Ned pulled out of the driveway onto the street. Once they got going, the wind on her face felt refreshingly sharp in comparison to how cozy and warm the rest of her felt, bundled up in the plaid throw. Then the heat came on, warming her feet, and Randi decided the evening was off to a perfect start. It all seemed so wonderfully romantic.

The only problem with driving with the top down, she discovered, was that it made conversation difficult—the wind drowned out most of their words. Still, Ned tried. "Nice night," he yelled at one point.

"Beautiful," she agreed loudly.

They drove a little further. "You look nice," he yelled.

Randi gathered up her courage. "So do you."

They fell silent again, and she soon discovered this lack of conversation wasn't so bad. First dates were always awkward, she knew, and there was something relaxing about just riding next to him, with the fresh night air swirling around them.

At the same time Randi had realized something else about Ned that she had never suspected. Deep down, he was shy, maybe just as shy as she was. He just knew how to camouflage it better. Even though he seemed to have everything going for him, Ned had none of the tough-guy bravado that some of the other boys did. He was refreshingly low-key, and Randi suddenly realized how well his personality seemed to complement hers.

Although it was a twenty-minute drive to the restaurant, the trip passed by in a flash. Soon Ned was helping her out of the car, and she was walking through the restaurant's wide glass doors. As her eyes adjusted to the dim light, she could see the place was jammed. The hostess led them to an empty table in the back, and as they snaked through the aisles, Randi could feel everyone's eyes turning toward them. Gritting her teeth, she fixed a blank expression on her face, as if her being escorted by Ned was nothing out of the ordinary. But she knew her flaming cheeks gave her away.

Then they passed a rear table where two girls were huddled together, seemingly oblivious to everything else. As soon as they walked by, one of the girls looked at Ned. It was Vicki Greene, Randi noticed. Then the other girl turned her head, and Randi's heart sank. Vicki's confidante was Linda Olgeirson, Ned's ex-girlfriend.

Randi saw Ned and Linda exchange a brief, charged look, then everyone turned their eyes away, pretending they hadn't seen each other. Randi couldn't help but wonder what Ned was thinking right then. The rumor she had heard was that Linda had broken up with him, not the other way around. Did Ned still like her? Randi wondered. Did he wish he was with Linda instead of her?

If he did, it didn't show on his face. As he sat down and took the menu the hostess handed him, he didn't seem to have a care in the world. Flipping open the menu, he announced in a friendly voice, "I'm starved."

"Me too," Randi said with a smile. Maybe things would be all right after all.

Chapter Seven

As the busboy cleared the dishes, Randi stared dreamily at the flickering candle on the table. So far the date had been perfect— the more time she spent with Ned, the more comfortable she felt. Ned was different than she had imagined. He was quiet and modest, almost gentle. Even more thrilling, he seemed genuinely interested in her, asking her a lot of questions and listening intently to her answers. And of course, there was the warm look in his deep blue eyes. . . .

He broke into her thoughts abruptly. "I did promise to help you with your speech tonight," he began. "Maybe we could talk about it a little now."

Her class speech couldn't be further from her thoughts, but Randi smiled gamely. She trusted Ned enough now to be honest about her problems with the speech. "I haven't definitely decided on a topic yet," she said. He nodded in understanding, and she realized that this admission wasn't such a terrible thing after all. "The only thing I've got so far is something about the Grand Canyon," she continued.

"You told me you went there on a trip, right?"

"Yeah, last summer," she said. "We visited my uncle in Flagstaff. The Grand Canyon is about an hour's drive from there." Just talking about it brought back happy memories, and she smiled. "We had the nicest lunch in this hotel called the Bright Angel Lodge. It was so pretty and rustic. It's the oldest hotel in the canyon," she added, warming to the subject.

"What else did you like?" he asked.

"Well, I thought the canyon was interesting and all, but it was the settlement around it that really fascinated me. The lodges and souvenir stands were built in connection with the Sante Fe Railway. That's what made the Grand Canyon a big tourist spot in the first place."

"When the railroad came through?" Ned asked, sounding intrigued.

Randi hesitated, not understanding his sudden enthusiasm. "Uh-huh."

"That's it!" he exclaimed. "The topic for your speech! How the Grand Canyon became a tourist attraction. How the railroad changed it forever."

"Do you think so?" Randi felt a flicker of excitement run through her. Maybe this wouldn't be so bad after all.

"I do, yeah. I think it's very interesting," Ned declared.

He was so convincing that Randi began to consider the idea seriously. "I guess that is more interesting than talking about how the canyon was formed by the Colorado River over millions of years," she admitted.

"You can put that part in there too," Ned explained, his blue eyes flashing. "It's interesting, but the story behind how it became a tourist attraction is even better. And that," he added, his voice taking on a deeper tone, "is what successful public speaking is all about—being interested in your subject. If you're really into it, it comes across."

"You sound like Mr. Harvey," Randi teased lightly.

To her astonishment, Ned blushed. "Sorry," he said. "Sometimes I get a little preachy when I feel strongly about things."

"You don't have to apologize," she said quickly, mortified to have embarrassed him. "I like people who have definite opinions," she added softly.

Ned smiled crookedly, melting Randi's heart completely.

The evening had passed too quickly, Randi decided with a sigh as Ned pulled his MG into the driveway. It seemed to Randi as if they had only been gone a few minutes. She wished the night could last forever.

Easing the car to a smooth stop, Ned switched off the ignition. He slowly turned to face her and took a deep breath. "I had a good time tonight," he said formally.

"Me too." Her heart felt like it was about to burst.

He looked down at his hands and self-consciously cleared his throat. "I wanted to ask you something," he said, with an awkward attempt at a smile that only endeared him even more to Randi. He was just as nervous as she was! "I was wondering if you've made any plans for the Christmas dance."

"Plans?" she repeated, even though she knew exactly what he meant.

"I mean, like a date."

Randi stared down at her lap. "No." It came out so softly that she wondered if he even heard it.

"The thing is," he continued, "I'd like to take you, but I'm on the committee that's hanging all the decorations, so I have to be there early to hang them and then stay afterward to take them down. There's a PTA meeting the next day and they need the gym."

Randi felt confused. Was he asking her or not?

"Anyway," Ned went on, "I can't pick you up or take you home, but maybe I can, um, see you there?"

I can't believe this! Randi thought. "Umm, that would be nice," she said, looking into his eyes briefly.

"Great," Ned said with a relieved sigh. He walked her up the short path in front of her house and when they got to the front door, Randi's heart started¡to pound. Even though she hadn't allowed herself to think about it before, now she was wondering if he was going to kiss her good night.

She fumbled in her bag for her keys, trying to think of something to say. "Well, thanks again," she began politely.

"Sure," he murmured, rubbing the back of his neck. "Well, good night." He seemed about to turn around when all at once that same searching look came over his face, and then she knew he was going to kiss her.

"I really like you, you know," he murmured. Then he leaned forward and tentatively touched her arm. Everything seemed to be going in slow motion as though in a dream. Surprising herself, Randi tilted her head automatically, as if kissing him was the most natural thing in the world. When their lips met, Randi felt herself tremble. Even though the kiss was short—they both pulled away shyly at the same time—it was as magical as Randi had dreamed it would be.

" 'Night," Ned whispered huskily, and after a half-wave, he vanished into the night. Randi went inside and leaned against the door, sighing dreamily as she watched his car pull away. She would remember this night forever!

"I want to hear everything," Amy said as Randi came into her room the following morning. They were still working on the crepe paper poinsettias for the dance.

"Boy, you certainly haven't wasted any time since the last time I was over here." Randi grinned as she looked around in amazement. Amy's room looked as if a florist shop had exploded in it. Paper flowers were piled up everywhere. She could barely see the plush white carpet that covered the floor, except in the narrow aisles Amy had left to walk through. Randi stepped carefully along the path that led to the bed, and Amy cleared a place for her to sit.

"Well, I've hardly left this room. I was

even working on the flowers last night. But I haven't been able to get much done today. My phone's been ringing all morning," Amy added with a sly grin. "I guess I was the only person in the world who wasn't at Shakey's last night."

"So what is everyone saying?" Randi asked as a blush warmed her cheeks.

"They're all dying to know what's going on between you and Ned," Amy said. She added with a giggle, "So am I."

"We've only gone out once," Randi protested. "Why is everybody making such a big deal about it?"

"Because it's *Ned Taggert*, that's why. Mister Perfect. Everyone's dream. Now, come on, tell me. How did it go?"

Randi quickly recounted the evening, lingering on the drive over with the top of the car down, wrapped up in a blanket. This had struck her as the ultimate in romance.

"Wait a minute," Amy interrupted. "Slow down. I thought you told me you didn't like him that much."

"Well . . ." Randi traced her finger along the cording on Amy's bedspread. "I didn't think so," she said vaguely. "I guess I made a mistake." She thought of how wrong she had been about him when he had first given her that look in English class.

"Well, at least you're coming to your senses," Amy said. "Are you going out with him again?"

"Well, kind of."

"Did he ask you to the dance?" Amy asked breathlessly.

"Kind of."

"He *did*?" Amy squealed. "Randi, that's fantastic!"

"He *sort of* asked me," Randi repeated, not wanting to make it sound like more than it was. "He's got to be there early to hang the decorations and then stay late to take them down, so he's not driving me," she explained. "I'm just going to, um, see him there."

"Oh," Amy said, faintly disappointed. "Still, that's very exciting. I'm sure he'll be with you all night."

Randi breathed a sign of relief. She hadn't been sure how Amy would react to all this, but she actually seemed happy for her.

"I wish you had a date, though," Randi added, feeling bad for her friend. "Then it would be perfect."

Amy suddenly turned her attention to the pile of crepe paper lying in front of her and began to twist and fold it rapidly. "Actually there's something I haven't told you yet," she began bashfully, sliding the pipe cleaners over to Randi without looking up.

"What?" Randi looked at her, waiting.

Amy yanked the flower she was working on into a knot. "You're not the only one who's meeting someone at the dance," she confessed. She tossed the flower on a pile at the foot of the bed. "I'm meeting Rusty."

Randi's mouth fell open in surprise. "That's terrific," she said encouragingly. "What changed your mind?"

"Well, I thought I'd give him another chance," Amy said. "Partly because of what you've been telling me. Maybe I do like him," she added in a tiny voice. "Anyway, he's not taking me either, I'm just going to meet him there. If it doesn't work out, I don't want to be stuck riding home with him."

"I knew he'd call you!" Randi said triumphantly.

"He didn't call me," she said flatly.

"You called him?" Randi asked, trying not to sound too incredulous.

"Yup," Amy said breezily. "It's not like I hardly know the guy, after all. I mean, I'll always be friends with him." She put down the flower she was working on and tipped her head to meet Randi's gaze. "I was so petrified," she admitted.

"Well, it's not important *how* it happened. The main thing is that you're going to meet him, right?" Randi said.

"I guess," Amy sighed. "Sometimes I wish you hadn't talked me into this, though. It could be a real disaster."

"It's going to work out, you'll see," Randi promised.

The two girls got busy on the flowers, and for a while, the only sound in the room was the rustling of the crepe paper.

"I've got an idea for my speech and I want to know what you think," Randi said a few minutes later. She quickly explained what she and Ned had come up with.

Amy tapped her chin thoughtfully. "It's kind of strange, but I like it," she finally announced. "When you originally said the Grand Canyon, at first I thought it was going to be about rocks and geology and all that."

"That could be boring."

"It *is* kind of predictable. But at least then no one would be paying any attention, and you wouldn't have any reason to get nervous," Amy pointed out.

"I know, but since it counts as part of my English grade and all . . ." Randi paused. "And anyway, I have to get over this problem."

"You sound sort of psyched about the whole thing," Amy observed.

"I guess I am," Randi admitted. "Ned's getting me psyched. He's going to coach me."

"That's great."

Randi nodded her head, suddenly feeling a bit uncertain. There was only so much Ned could do. The thought of standing up in front of the whole assembly still tied her stomach up in knots.

Between working on her speech and getting ready for Christmas, Randi barely had a minute to think about the dance. The days flew by, and before she knew it, it was the day before the dance. Randi couldn't believe the time had whizzed by so quickly. Just think, she told herself, tomorrow night you'll be at the dance with Ned!

"I guess that's it," Amy said, panting as they loaded Amy's brother's van with the last of the flowers for delivery to the gym. It seemed as if they had made a hundred trips up and down the stairs from her room to the car. "I guess the next time I'll see you will be tomorrow night."

"Um-hmmm." Randi nodded. The thought of it all was making her a little nervous.

"How did your dress come out?" Amy asked. She hadn't seen it yet, although Randi had described it in complete detail.

"Wait till you see it," Randi said, trying to work up some enthusiasm. "Pick you up at eight tomorrow, okay?" Randi's mother had agreed to drive them over.

"I can't wait!" Amy exclaimed, slamming the van door shut. "It's going to be the best dance ever, right?"

Randi swallowed, ignoring the nervous flutter in her stomach. "Right," she said.

Chapter Eight

At precisely eight o'clock the following night, Randi gingerly walked up the path leading to the massive front door of the Bishops' house. She felt like a different person—nothing like the usual jeans-and-sneakers Randi. Her new dressed swished when she walked, and her high heels clicked on the stone walk. After carefully negotiating the porch steps, she was just about to ring the bell when the door swung open.

Amy was waiting there, her eyes dancing excitedly. "Well?" she said eagerly. "Let's see it." Randi obediently shed her overcoat, and

Amy gasped. "Oh, Randi, it's even more gorgeous than I thought! I love the color."

"Thanks." Amy's enthusiasm was catching, helping her ignore the nervousness she felt about meeting Ned at the dance. She'd spoken to him briefly at school and during English class, but he was always rushing off to some meeting or event. "Let me see your dress. Turn around," Randi instructed with a smile.

"Do you like it?"

"It's fantastic," Randi replied. Amy's dress, an ice-blue satin with puffed sleeves and a square neckline, was truly a knockout. The finishing touch was her hair, which she'd worn up, a single gardenia pinned above her left ear. The total effect was very elegant and sophisticated. "Rusty's going to die when he sees you," Randi gushed.

"Well . . ." Amy sounded doubtful.

"He will. I know it. Now you have to promise to have a good time tonight," Randi said firmly. "No matter what."

"I promise," Amy grinned sheepishly.

"Oh, I better warn you," Randi murmured as Amy was putting her coat on. "My mom's car broke down this afternoon. *Charles* is driving us over."

"So?" Amy paused, one arm in her coat.

"What's the big deal? You make it sound so awful. I happen to like Charles."

"I was just telling you," Randi said defensively.

"Okay!" Amy bugged her eyes comically. "I'm prepared."

It was a little difficult getting into the backseat of Charles's Toyota with long dresses on, but they managed. "Hello, Mrs. Hinton," Amy said once she got in. "Hello, Mr. Payne," she added, shooting Randi a significant look.

"You remember Amy, don't you, Charles?" Randi's mother asked.

"We've met before." Charles nodded and smiled. "We met once when you were visiting Randi, about two months ago, right, Amy?"

"That's right!" Amy flushed, obviously pleased that he'd remembered. "It's nice to see you again." She pushed the toe of her shoe against Randi's leg lightly, and Randi smiled against her will. Amy had made her point. Charles wasn't so bad after all.

It was a short ride to Brockenborough Prep from the Bishops' house, which was located nearby in the exclusive section of Northhaven. After agreeing to be picked up at twelve-thirty—a time that had been set after some hard bargaining between both girls and their mothers—Randi and Amy headed across the parking lot toward the gym. The entryway twinkled with flashing white and blue Christmas lights, and the muffled sound of a live band drifted through the cold night air. The party had begun.

After checking their coats, they went straight to the ladies' room. To get there, they had to snake around the back of the gym to the entrance of the girls' locker room.

"It feels weird walking through here all dressed up," Amy murmured as they passed the rows of lockers, the corridor brightly lit by fluorescent lights.

"Not exactly 'A Christmas Fantasy,' " Randi replied dryly.

There wasn't anyone in the bathroom, and Amy positioned herself in front of one of the mirrors, tugging at her dress to make sure it wasn't bunched up after the cramped car ride. "Are you nervous?" she asked, then paused, a suspicious look on her face. "Is my hair staying up in back?" she said in the next breath.

Randi smiled and nodded. She *was* a little nervous, but she knew Amy had the right attitude. It was just a party, after all. It would be nice to dance with Ned once or twice. But she shouldn't expect anything more, she told herself. He hadn't *really* asked her to be his date.

"Can I give you some advice?" Amy's voice cut into her thoughts.

"I *am* a little nervous—" Randi began.

"Remember our promise," Amy interrupted. "Just relax and have fun tonight, okay?"

"Do I look too nervous?"

"No," Amy said. "As a matter of fact, you happen to look great. That dress is incredible."

"Thanks." Randi blinked at her image in the mirror. There was a short pause, and then she asked, "Can I give *you* some advice?" Amy nodded. "Give Rusty a chance tonight, all right?"

Amy smiled ruefully. "Okay. You're really serious about this, aren't you?"

"I won't give up until you two are back together," Randi said. "I always thought Rusty was a really nice guy." Squaring her shoulders, she led Amy out of the girls' room and into the gym.

As they moved around the vast gym floor, Randi couldn't believe how magical the room looked now that it was decorated.

"I can't believe we made all those," Amy said, pointing up at the garlands of poinsettias that were gracefully strung from the rafters. "But they do look pretty good, don't they?"

"It was worth it," Randi agreed absent-mindedly. She hadn't really been looking around at the decorations at all—she had been looking around for Ned. To her disappointment, there was no sign of him anywhere.

"Want something to drink?" Amy asked. Randi was about to agree when Ned appeared at her side out of nowhere. Her heart did a flip-flop.

"You look terrific," was the first thing he said.

"You too," she breathed, studying him quickly. It was the first time she had ever seen him in a tuxedo, and the sight took her breath away. Ned looked so mature, so handsome.

Ned said hello to Amy, and Randi suddenly realized that Rusty had also joined their group. Their dates weren't wasting any time, she thought with a happy surge of confidence.

After some small talk, Amy and Rusty faded away to join the crowd by the punch bowl, and Randi felt a rush of adrenaline shoot through her. They were alone now.

"So . . ." Ned began, tugging at his bright red bow tie as if it were too tight. "What do you want to do? Feel like dancing?"

"Umm . . . in a minute," Randi replied. What she really wanted to do was just talk to him for a while, get to know him all over again. That would help take away her nervousness. Out of the corner of her eye she noticed that the people passing by seemed to be looking them over carefully. *Let them stare,* she thought. *I know I look pretty nice.*

"How about some punch, then?" he asked.

Randi glanced over at the punch bowl, where Amy and Rusty were in the middle of what looked like a very private conversation, and decided it would be best to give them some time alone. "Umm, no. Actually, I *am* in the mood to dance," she said, hoping she didn't sound too fickle.

"Okay." He seemed full of energy as he took her arm and led her toward the floor. Suddenly a voice called out, "Ned!" They both turned toward the bleachers behind them where the voice seemed to be coming from.

"Ned!" Vicki Greene yelled again, beckoning to him, a camera in her hand. "Come here a sec. I want to get a picture of you with the rest of the yearbook staff." Randi saw all the other members standing there, posed around a sled full of presents, Brockenborough Prep's annual donation to a local charity.

Ned sighed. "I hate having my picture taken," he confessed to Randi. "Sorry about this. I'll be right back, okay?"

"Okay," Randi agreed, silently wondering who had appointed Vicki official photographer for the dance.

She pushed this thought out of her mind and tried to look around the room casually, sneaking little peeks at Ned every now and then. When Vicki's flash went off, Ned stepped away, only to be stopped again by Vicki. Over the noise and the music, Randi heard something about solo shots.

Ned caught Randi's eye and gestured helplessly. She smiled in return, acting as if it didn't matter, and edged closer to the dance floor, not wanting to seem too helpless without him. Nodding hello to Mrs. Grandy, her economics teacher, she pretended to be engrossed in the people gyrating on the dance floor, but inside she was seething. Vicki seemed intent on keeping Ned over there for as long as possible.

Her gaze moved to the punch bowl and then around the crowd. Amy and Rusty were nowhere to be seen. Casually she let her eyes travel back to Ned. He was sitting on the bleachers waiting for his turn to be photographed, deep in an intense conversation with Jimmy Vardy. He seemed to have forgotten her completely.

Randi shifted her weight uncomfortably from one foot to the other. How could he leave her standing there like this? she wondered. She tried to focus her attention on the band, whose name, Out of Control, was stenciled on the drums. Randi couldn't decide whether they were any good or not, but the crowd seemed to love them. She watched the dancers for a few minutes and then let her eyes move back to Ned.

Vicki had finally gotten around to taking his picture and had posed him in the entryway, which was decorated with garlands of pine branches intertwined with pine cones and red ribbons. All at once, Randi realized that Linda Olgeirson, Ned's ex-girlfriend, was standing beside Vicki. Linda looked gorgeous, Randi thought with a sinking feeling.

After some prodding by Vicki, Linda moved next to Ned to have their picture taken together. "Go ahead," Vicki called out, loud enough for Randi to hear. Then Vicki pointed at something suspended from the ceiling above the couple.

To Randi's horror, Vicki was pointing to a spring of mistletoe. She watched dumbstruck as Ned kissed Linda. Slipping her arms around his neck, Linda kissed him back—for what seemed like a long, long time. Randi snapped her head away and stared blankly at the wall. How could he do this to her? It was just as she'd suspected—she really wasn't his date after all. But what kind of game was he playing? Unable to resist one last glance in his direction, she saw him posing for another picture with Linda. They sure looked cozy, Randi thought. Linda still had her arms around Ned, and her head was resting on his shoulder. And Ned didn't exactly look like he was desperate to get away.

Randi's heart turned to stone. Blinking back the sudden tears, she plunged into the crowd on the dance floor and blindly made her way across the room. All she wanted to do was get away from him. The entrance to the girls' locker room came into view, and without hesitating, she slipped inside, hurried past the lockers into the bathroom, and closed herself in one of the stalls. She leaned against the door and buried her head in her hands. How could this be happening? she thought wildly. How could she have allowed herself to think a boy like Ned Taggert really cared about her?

She wasn't sure how long she stood there,

but it seemed like a long time. She was finally shaken out of her thoughts when two girls came into the bathroom and started talking. At first Randi didn't pay much attention to what they were saying, but then she heard her name mentioned.

"I heard he was going out with Randi Hinton now," one girl said.

"I don't think so," another voice replied. "Linda Olgeirson told me he still likes her. She said they just had a temporary misunderstanding and that he only asked Randi out to make her jealous."

Randi froze. And she had trusted Ned! "Do you think they're going to get back together?"

"I don't know. Linda sure seems to think so. And what Linda wants, she usually gets."

"That would explain things," the first girl admitted. "I mean, why he's been drooling over Linda all night when rumor had it he was seeing Randi."

"Has Ned really been dating Randi?" the other girl asked after a moment.

"Where have you been? They were at Shakey's together two weeks ago. It's all people are talking about."

There was a long pause. "Well, I don't get it," Randi tried to peek through the crack in the door to see who was talking, but all she could see was a sliver of white dress.

Then one of the girls asked, "Are you ready?" and suddenly they were gone. Randi angrily left the stall and inspected herself in front of the mirror. The conversation she'd overheard seemed to jolt her into action. *You look fine*, she repeated to herself, inspecting her reflection critically. *You can't hide in the bathroom all night. Pull yourself together, go out there, and confront Ned.* Digging into her bag for her blush, she began furiously dusting her cheeks.

A moment later Amy breezed in, all smiles. "I don't believe it," she said ecstatically, giving Randi a wild hug. "You were absolutely right!"

"About what?" Randi blinked at her in surprise.

"About Rusty," Amy said dreamily, pulling a comb from her purse and gently touching up her hairdo. "About giving him another chance. He's been saying the most incredible things to me all night. Stuff about how much he missed me, and how he really cares for me. I never realized . . ." She paused, a look of absolute bliss on her face.

"That's great." Randi tried to force some

enthusiasm into her voice. At least someone was having a good time tonight, she thought miserably.

Amy's comb froze in midair as she studied her friend's reflection in the mirror. "What's the matter with you?" she asked suspiciously. "What are you doing in here anyway?"

"What do you think?" Randi tried to sound nonchalant. "I'm fixing my makeup."

"Look at your cheeks!" Amy exclaimed. "You have on so much blush, they look like they're on fire."

Randi stole a glance in the mirror and swallowed hard. She had been so absorbed in her thoughts that she hadn't paid attention to what she had been doing. "Well, I was a little upset," she confessed.

Amy's high spirits seemed to vanish in an instant. "What's the matter?" she asked softly.

Randi bit her lip, and then the whole story about Ned and Vicki and Linda and the conversation she'd overheard came pouring out. Amy listened attentively, nodding now and then. After Randi finished, she sighed. "Well . . ." she began. "I didn't want to say anything, but I did see him dancing with Vicki Greene just now. *She* probably asked *him*, though," Amy quickly added.

Randi's shoulders slumped. "You see what I mean? He really didn't ask me to this dance. I was only fooling myself. I feel like such a dope."

"That's not true, Randi," Amy shot back. "He was just caught up with taking pictures for the yearbook. And even if what you heard is true, you'll never know unless you get out there and give him a chance. He can't explain things to you if you're hiding in the girls' room all night."

Randi considered this reluctantly, knowing that it was true. "Just let me fix my face," she said, reaching for a tissue and studying her reflection. "I look like a clown," she added wryly, and wiped off the excess blush.

Amy shook her head. "You look great. If Ned doesn't appreciate you, then *he's* a clown."

Rusty was waiting patiently by the locker room entrance when they came out. Randi could see the excitement in both their eyes, and she wanted to feel happy for them, but it was hard. She was too preoccupied with her problem with Ned. If she got him alone, what would she do? she wondered wildly.

Realizing that Amy and Rusty wanted to be alone, she excused herself and casually made her way over to Brenda Chen. They were telling each other about their holiday plans when suddenly Randi spotted Ned out of the corner of her eye. He was standing next to Vicki Greene and two of the other cheerleaders, laughing. He must have felt her looking at him, because their eyes met for a split second. Randi quickly looked away. She refused to look at him like some kind of lovesick puppy. He'd humiliated her enough already. A lump was forming in her throat and Randi excused herself from Brenda and headed for the opposite side of the gym. What had started out as the most perfect night of her life was quickly turning into a nightmare.

Chapter Nine

The rest of the weekend after the dance passed in a blur of misery. All Randi could think about was Ned and how disappointed she felt. She was usually very wary of people, but she had really trusted him. And now it looked like he had only used her to make his ex-girlfriend jealous. Still, a little voice inside asked why she had avoided him all night. Wouldn't it have been smarter to seek him out later and demand an explanation instead of running away and hiding? She hated confrontations—but wouldn't it be better to know the truth? Why was she such a coward? she wondered.

These thoughts loomed larger on Monday

morning. Would any of the kids be talking about her? As she was walking to school, she suddenly remembered that she would see him in English at third bell, and her heart sank. Could she maintain her cool? The picture of him kissing Linda at the dance was as firmly set in her mind as if she had taken a picture and hung it on the wall.

Just as she passed through the stone lions at the entrance to Brockenborough Prep's driveway, Randi heard a car coming up behind her and automatically stepped aside to let it pass. She wasn't paying much attention to who it was until she realized the car had slowed to a crawl right beside her. Out of the corner of her eye she saw a flash of red that was distinctly familiar.

Her heart started to pound in panic. Who else drove a red MG?

"Hi!" Ned called out. His cheeks were red from the cold, but as usual, he was driving with the top down.

"Hello, Ned," she managed past the lump in her throat. He was wearing a pair of mirrored sunglasses, which made it impossible to read the expression in his eyes. Still, he seemed just as calm and relaxed as ever, as if nothing out of the ordinary had happened Saturday night. How dare he be so relaxed?

she fumed. Just the sight of him raised a storm of angry emotions in her. She quickly looked away.

Randi walked silently into the parking lot, the MG creeping along beside her. "What happened to you the other night?" Ned finally asked. "You left pretty early."

She didn't know what to say, but the way he put it stung her. "You seemed kind of *busy*," she said, staring at a thatch of dead-looking grass on the side of the drive.

"Are you mad at me?" he asked quietly.

Randi was about to reply when she was cut off by the toot of a car horn behind them. It was a group of Ned's friends, all crammed into Jimmy Vardy's Jeep. In the backseat she spotted Craig Ambler, and sitting next to him was Vicki Greene. "Great—just what I need now," she mumbled under her breath.

"Get a move on, Ned, old boy," Jimmy Vardy called out good-naturedly. "We haven't got all day."

"Yeah, either give the *poor* girl a ride or don't," Vicki Greene added, tossing her head at Randi.

Randi flushed and looked at Ned. His expression seemed blank as he said, "Get in," making it more a demand than a request.

Randi mutely obeyed. She didn't want to make a scene in front of everyone.

He pulled into a parking space a moment later and cut the motor. "You never answered my question," he said.

"What question?" she murmured. Her mind was whirling. Not only was she having a hard time talking to Ned, but she realized they now had an audience. Jimmy Vardy had pulled his Jeep into a place two spaces away.

"Are you mad at me?" Ned repeated.

"Why should I be?" she shot back, flipping her hair over her shoulder. "It's not like I was really your *date* or anything."

Ned just shrugged. After a moment he said, "I thought maybe you were mad about what happened at the dance."

Well, if you had paid me a little attention, I wouldn't be, Randi thought angrily, biting her lower lip. Out of the corner of her eye she saw Vicki Greene climbing out of the Jeep. Suddenly all she wanted to do was get out of there.

"If this had anything to do with Linda . . ." he began unsteadily.

"I don't care what you do with Linda!" Randi exploded, wishing instantly that she could take it back. The words seemed to have popped out of her mouth against her will. She didn't want to give away how much she had counted on this date, and how much she'd been hurt.

"They set me up with that mistletoe, you know," Ned explained. "Linda and Vicki Greene. Just to embarrass me."

"You certainly didn't seem *that* embarrassed." Again she seemed to have lost control of her tongue.

"You *are* mad, aren't you?" Ned said ruefully. Shaking his head, he took off his sunglasses and stared at her with his deep blue eyes. She hated to admit it, but just the sight of them nearly melted her on the spot.

"Hey guys," an overly cheerful voice piped up behind them. "What's up?" It was Vicki, a big grin on her face. If she could tell that Ned and Randi were having a private discussion, Vicki blithely ignored it. She stopped by Ned's side of the car and leaned back against the door, as if settling down for a long, friendly conversation. "Great party Saturday night, wasn't it?" she remarked.

Ned looked completely disgusted. "We were just discussing that," he said, shooting Randi a pleading look.

Randi ignored his plea. "I've got to run, you guys," she said. *Coward!* a little voice inside her said. "I've got to get something to

Mr. Harvey before first bell." Fumbling with the door handle, she got out of the car.

"See you, Randi," Vicki purred triumphantly.

"Can I walk you?" Ned asked, looking up at her and then down at his hands.

"I-I-I . . ." Randi stammered, feeling that familiar hot feeling creeping over her face. How could she stutter at a time like this? she wondered in disgust. "I've got to run," she managed to say, and without another word she turned and sped away. She had to get out of there before she turned any redder.

By the time she entered Monroe Hall, she was a complete wreck, and she went straight to the girls' room. A glance in the mirror confirmed her worst suspicions—she was red as a beet. Just thinking about Ned, not to mention the condescending look on Vicki Greene's face, made her heart race angrily.

Randi glanced at her watch and saw that it was three-thirty. She looked down Prospect Street anxiously, but there was still no sign of Amy anywhere. Where could she be? Randi wondered. One thing Amy insisted on was always being on time. She usually drove Randi crazy about it. But today she was late. They had agreed to meet in front of Lee's Photo

Supply at three o'clock, and Randi was beginning to get concerned.

She had been staring at the camera equipment arranged in the display windows for over half an hour, but she wasn't really taking anything in. She just couldn't take her mind off the problem that had been gnawing at her all day—her disastrous conversation with Ned earlier that morning in the parking lot. How could she have been such an idiot? He had been trying to apologize to her—or at least explain—and she had completely blown him off. She at least owed him a chance to tell her what had happened. And he really had seemed sorry. But now he was ignoring her altogether. At third-period English class, he didn't even glance at her as he took his seat, and even though she'd hung around her desk at the end of class, he'd made no attempt to talk to her. Randi had slunk out of the class feeling disgusted with herself.

All at once Amy appeared, darting around the corner breathlessly.

"Where have you been?" Randi demanded. "I was getting worried."

"Sorry I'm late," Amy apologized. "I was, um, with Rusty."

"Really?" Randi said, studying her friend carefully. Amy had a vibrant glow in her

113

cheeks and a sparkle in her eyes that Randi hadn't seen in weeks. She forced herself to feel happy for her friend. At least one of them was in love, she thought.

"You were right about him all along," Amy bubbled excitedly. "I must have been crazy to have broken up with him. He's the only boy who understands me. He makes me feel so . . ." Amy flung her arms around exuberantly, searching for the right word. "So . . . I don't know. I can't explain it."

"I told you." Randi grinned, a bittersweet sensation passing over her. *When will it happen to me?* she wondered wistfully, thinking briefly of Ned. She shook the thought off. The main thing was that Amy was happy.

"So . . ." Amy sighed expansively, turning to the display window. "Have you seen anything here that we can't live without?"

Randi turned back to the glass. Even though she had been staring at the photo equipment for some time, she had been so lost in her own thoughts that nothing had registered. She examined the window again. "I see the lens you were thinking about getting," she said after a moment, pointing to a wide-angle lens that Amy had wanted.

"Anything else?" Amy asked merrily. She was certainly in a good mood.

"There are some pretty neat filters there." Randi gestured toward the lower corner of the window.

"Well, come on, then," Amy said, taking her by the arm and dragging her through the entrance.

Half an hour later the two girls left the store, laden with packages. "Well." Amy exhaled loudly. "I certainly feel a lot better. There's nothing like shopping to cheer you up," she added.

"I thought you were in a pretty good mood to start with," Randi observed.

"I wasn't referring to myself," Amy said, raising her eyebrows significantly. "I was hoping this would cheer *you* up."

Randi's shoulders slumped. All of her frustration about Ned came rushing back over her. "Is it that obvious?" she asked in a forlorn voice.

"Randi, I'm your best friend!" Amy exclaimed. "Best friends can tell that kind of thing about each other." She paused and pointed to an empty bench near the entrance to City Park. "Let's go sit over there. I need a rest after all that shopping," she added, trying to sound cheerful.

Randi followed her halfheartedly. She knew

that Amy was only trying to be helpful. Besides, maybe talking about it would make her feel better.

"So, what's wrong?" Amy got right to the point once they had arranged themselves and the shopping bags on the wooden bench. "I bet it's got something to do with Mister Perfect."

"I ran into Ned this morning," Randi began, studying her nails. "And I know I blew it. I blew it completely."

"How?" Amy demanded.

"I think he was kind of trying to apologize about the dance and all, and I didn't give him a chance. Why am I such a dope?" she said, shaking her head.

"At least he was trying to apologize," Amy pointed out.

"He was probably really just making excuses. You know, blaming Vicki and Linda. He didn't even look that upset—or that sorry."

"Oh, that's just the way guys are. They'd rather die than show any emotion," Amy insisted in her experienced-woman voice. "So what did you say to him?"

"That's the worst part," Randi murmured. "Vicki Greene came over right in the middle of our conversation and butted in. And I ran away," she added in a tiny voice. She was embarrassed to admit it, but she knew she could tell Amy anything.

"I can't stand Vicki," Amy said loyally. "Why did you run away, though? You should have stood your ground and made Vicki go away."

"Well," Randi said with a sigh, "I was starting to turn red and get all flustered. You know the way I am." She hung her head miserably.

Amy didn't say anything for a long moment. Then she slowly began to shake her head. "You know, Randi, I don't know how many times I've got to tell you this, but you are a *terrific* person—and much more popular than you think you are. You're much nicer than Vicki Greene, that's for sure. And I think Ned knows it, too. That's why he was interested in you."

Randi didn't say anything, warmed by her friend's comforting words. Still, some questions remained. "Then why didn't he pay any attention to me at the dance?" she asked stubbornly. "And what about what those girls said in the bathroom?"

"Forget about that stupid gossip. Maybe Ned really *was* set up with those yearbook photos. And maybe Ned didn't spend time with you later because you were hiding all night," Amy said firmly. "And we left early."

Randi sighed again. There was no point in arguing with Amy about this topic. Deep down, Randi knew she could be right. "When I talk to you about it, it seems so easy. Why can't I see things that way on my own? And why can't I ever speak up for myself?"

"Because you just don't have enough self-confidence," Amy said. "It's that simple. How's your speech coming, by the way?"

"What has that got to do with anything?"

"Randi, don't you get it?" Amy questioned. "It's really the same thing. Not being able to speak in public and not being able to talk to the best-looking guy in school is the same thing. No self-confidence!" She raised her palms in the air in mock exasperation.

Randi couldn't help but laugh. "I'm working on it," she said gamely, but she felt more lost than ever.

Chapter Ten

"The holidays seem to creep up faster and faster every year," Randi's mother mused, shaking her head ruefully. "I can't believe Christmas is just three days away." She stepped back to inspect the wreath of pine cones and holly, finished with a shiny red bow, that they had just hung on the front door. "Is this up straight?"

Randi stepped back to study it critically. Their decorations were going up a little late this year, but her mother had been so busy between her job and the real estate course she was taking that they hadn't had the time until now. "The wreath looks fine," she told her mother.

"I think we both deserve a cup of hot cider." Mrs. Hinton smiled and, slinging her arm over Randi's shoulders affectionately, led the way back inside.

The house smelled like pine needles, and as they passed through the living room, Randi saw the colored lights on the tree flashing merrily. Just the sight of it sent a tingle of delight through her, bringing back fond memories of past Christmases. The holidays always made her feel even closer to her mother. They always made her feel so sentimental.

In the kitchen Mrs. Hinton bustled over to the stove where the spiced cider had been simmering and poured them each a steaming mug. "Mmm!" she exclaimed, after taking a sip. "It's good, but be careful, honey. It's hot."

Randi smiled affectionately. Her mom would never change; she was always worrying about her. There had been a time a few years back when this had bugged Randi. It seemed as if her mother didn't think she was capable of doing anything by herself. But lately Randi had begun to realize this was just her mother's way of showing her how much she loved her.

"So . . ." Mrs. Hinton continued, taking a seat next to Randi at the kitchen table. "Is there anything special you'd like for Christmas dinner? I've already stocked up on cranberry sauce," she added, her eyes twinkling. Cranberry sauce had been one of Randi's favorite holiday treats since she was a child.

"Whatever you like," Randi said. "You don't have to knock yourself out for just the two of us," she added, then paused. Would it be just the two of them? she suddenly wondered. What if Charles had been invited?

"We should make it nice anyway," her mother protested, blowing on her mug to cool the cider. "It *is* Christmas, after all." A faraway look settled over her face. "I only wish we lived closer to your Uncle David so the whole family could be together," she added wistfully. "That would be nice. But Arizona is so far away."

"So it's just going to be the two of us?" Randi asked in a small voice.

Her mother glanced over at her, clearly puzzled until she grasped Randi's meaning. "Just us, honey," she said. Mrs. Hinton hesitated, as if measuring her words. "I've, ah, been meaning to tell you something. I'm not going to be seeing Charles anymore. Dating him, I mean."

"You're not?" Randi interjected.

"No," her mother said quietly, pursing her lips. "I saw him a couple of nights ago, and we—no, *I*—decided that we should stop dating."

To Randi's astonishment, she felt a faint pang of regret shoot through her. Maybe all along she had liked Charles more than she was willing to admit. As a sad expression come over her mother's face, Randi's heart went out to her. "Gee, Mom," she whispered. "I'm really sorry. What happened?"

Mrs. Hinton sighed deeply. "It just wasn't working. Charles isn't the right man for me," she murmured. "He's a very nice person," she added quickly, "and I'm sure we will always be friends. But I'm simply not in love with him. I think the only reason I saw him for so long was because of you."

"*Me!*" Randi exclaimed, taken aback.

"I think you should have a father, honey," her mother replied softly, taking her hand. "You're missing out on so much with only one parent."

"I don't feel cheated," Randi murmured, blinking back sudden tears. "You more than make up for not having a father."

Soon Randi's mother was wiping away a

tear that had escaped from her eye. "Thank you for saying that, baby. That makes it all worth it." She paused, then asked sadly, "You liked Charles, didn't you?"

Randi swallowed. "Yes," she murmured automatically. Then it occurred to her that she really meant it. All at once she realized that she had never given Charles a fair chance; just as she hadn't really given Ned a chance to explain. She had only seen Charles as a threat, someone who would come between her and her mom. Now that he was out of the picture, Randi felt terribly guilty. She hadn't been fair at all—to Charles or to her mom. "The only thing I want is for you to be happy, Mom," she confessed. *And I promise myself to try not to be so afraid of people*, Randi added silently. *They're not all out to hurt me.*

Randi and her mother hugged, and Randi got up from the table to get them some tissues. After dabbing at her eyes and blowing her nose, Mrs. Hinton sipped her cider in silence for a while. Then, out of the blue, she asked, "Are you still dating Ned Taggert?"

Randi frowned. "No," she admitted. She hadn't told her mother much about Ned at all. Somehow she just couldn't. The whole subject, and the way she had acted, seemed too immature.

Mrs. Hinton evidently sensed that this wasn't a subject to be probed. "I guess Ned's just not the right person for you either," she said gently.

"Something like that," Randi agreed. Deep down, she couldn't make herself believe it, though.

"So what did you get?" Amy's voice rose excitedly over the phone. It was early Christmas morning, and Amy had wasted no time calling her. Like Randi and her mother, the Bishops had opened their presents on Christmas Eve.

"Well, I got this neat miniskirt, and a hair dryer, and some socks," Randi began. "I got my big present—my dress for the dance—before," she added. "What about you?"

Amy launched into a long, detailed description of the many gifts she'd received. It always took the Bishop family hours to unwrap all their presents, and it seemed to take nearly as long to describe them all. But Amy saved the best for last. "But that's not all. You'll never guess what my parents gave me." She sounded like she was about to burst.

"What?"

"A Jeep! A red Jeep. Can you believe it?"

"No kidding!" The thought of a certain other red car, Ned's MG, flashed through her mind, putting a damper on her mood. "That's great," she said, trying to sound enthusiastic.

She didn't fool Amy, though. "Speaking of sporty red cars," she said, her voice low and confidential, "I heard something about Ned that might interest you."

Randi forced herself to stay calm. "What's that?"

"I heard he still likes you."

Randi's heart began to beat faster in her chest. "I don't think so," she said quietly. "He hasn't made any effort to talk to me." *I can't allow myself to believe he likes me,* she thought.

"Well, that's not what Jimmy Vardy told me," Amy went on persistently. "Ned's evidently still upset about what happened at the dance. He's just kind of embarrassed to approach you."

"Well, he should be. What happened was *his* fault, not mine," Randi shot back, surprising herself at how harsh she sounded.

"Randi, for the trillionth time," Amy said, sounding exasperated. "You never gave him a chance that night. If you hadn't been hiding—"

"I really don't want to discuss this anymore." Randi's tone was abrupt. Then she caught herself. "I'm sorry," she said miserably. "I don't mean to sound so nasty."

Amy sighed. "It's okay. I was only trying to make you feel better," she said. "He still likes you, Rand. And *I* think you like him."

"I don't know what I feel," Randi said, her mind whirling. "Let's talk about something else."

"Such as?"

"Such as the parade," she said. An annual local event, the Brockenborough Founder's Day Parade was held two days after Christmas, and the two girls had planned to photograph it together this year. "What time do you want to meet?"

Amy didn't answer for a moment. "I guess I forgot to tell you," she said reluctantly. "I can't do it. We're going up to my grandmother's in Maine for the weekend, and Daddy will kill me if I don't go."

"That's all right," Randi replied, feeling disappointed. "I'll just take twice as many pictures," she added, trying to sound cheerful.

"I'm really sorry."

"Forget it," Randi said. "Talk to you later."

After she'd hung up, Randi couldn't forget

what Amy had said about Ned. It stuck in her mind no matter how hard she tried to ignore it. *Don't get your hopes up,* Randi warned herself. *You'll just be disappointed again.*

The morning of the Founder's Day Parade was unseasonably cold, with temperatures hovering around zero. This didn't shake Randi's determination to photograph it, however. She bundled herself up warmly and set out early to stake out a good vantage point.

Once outside, she wondered if she had overdone it on the layers. She was wearing a heavy sweater over a sweatshirt over a T-shirt, two pairs of tights, corduroy jeans, a wool cap, a long muffler, gloves, a down jacket, and high boots. With difficulty she reached for the camera slung over her shoulder and swung it up to her face. It was hard to maneuver because of all the layers of clothing she had on, but at least she was warm enough. Looking down, she realized that nothing she had on really matched, but she dismissed it with a shrug. Who could she possibly run into that she knew? she thought. Most everyone from school seemed to be away for the holidays.

Brockenborough Square had been decorated for the parade the night before, and Randi looked around at the result with approval. Red, white, and blue bunting was strung everywhere, on windows and over doorways, and along a series of specially constructed arches down Prospect Street. All of the merchants facing the avenue were flying American flags, and the Revolutionary War cannon in the center of the square, along with the war memorial behind it, was decorated with red and white flowers.

After taking a series of pictures of the cannon—Randi liked the way the colorful flowers stood out against the weathered iron—she moved back to Prospect Street. Just then she heard the high school marching band begin to tune up.

There weren't a lot of people on the street—the cold weather had taken care of that—and Randi easily found a good vantage point behind one of the blue sawhorses that the police had set up to block traffic along the route. As she waited for the parade to begin, she changed the lenses on her camera, using the wide-angle lens Amy had loaned her for the parade.

The parade began. The band struck up a lively version of "The Star-Spangled Banner" and moved down the street, their breath forming icy clouds in front of their faces. Randi squatted down for a low-angle shot of their approach and clicked off three rapid shots.

Next she photographed a group of baton twirlers leading off the Brockenborough High School Band, then hunched down again to get a low angle on the white convertible in which Mrs. Libby Tunstall was riding. When Mrs. Tunstall saw the camera, she smiled and waved majestically, and Randi cracked up. She was thankful that her camera kept Mrs. Tunstall from seeing her face.

Behind Mrs. Tunstall was a group of community board marchers, Randi's mother among them. Randi lifted her head when her mother's face came into focus and waved. "Over here, Mom!" she called out. She noticed there was no sign of Charles anywhere.

Her mother spotted her and smiled, waving her hand. "Getting a lot of good shots, honey?" she called.

"Yes. Let me get another one of you." As she clicked her camera, a male voice behind her startled her.

"Hello, Randi! Good morning, Paula," the man added in a louder voice, tipping his hat politely toward Mrs. Hinton in the parade. Randi realized with a start that it was Mr. Randolph, the publisher of the town newspaper, the *Brockenborough Clarion*, who was very well liked around town. To Randi's surprise, Mr. Randolph's eyes turned to her and remained there.

"So, Randi," he said, studying her camera as if he had an idea. "I've got a terrible problem today," he went on, getting right to the point. "My staff photographer is sick, and I don't have anyone to cover the parade. I'm not too good at this myself," he added, pointing to an Instamatic hanging rather forlornly from a frayed cord around his neck.

"You want m-me to photograph this for the *Clarion*?" Randi asked in disbelief.

"You just won a prize for your photography at BP, didn't you?" Mr. Randolph replied with a smile. "It seems to me that I read that in the paper a couple of weeks ago."

Randi nodded. "Uh, yes, I did. If you really want me to take some pictures for you, I'll try my best, Mr. Randolph," she said, swallowing hard. She hoped she was up to the task.

"I'm sure you'll do a splendid job," Mr. Randolph said. "And now if you'll excuse me, I've got to go take my place in the parade."

Randi remained frozen in the spot, still a bit stunned at her good luck. Even though the *Clarion* was only published three times a week and was pretty thin, Randi knew that it was read cover-to-cover by nearly everyone in town. Her pictures had appeared once before in the school newspaper, the *Brockenborough Bugle,* and that had been exciting, but it didn't compare with this.

Forcing herself out of her trance, she went at her task with a new sense of purpose. Before she'd been taking pictures for fun; now she had a more serious reason. Now every shot was composed with the front page of the *Clarion* in the back of her mind, and that thought made her even more inventive and creative. She darted along Prospect Street, snapping pictures of everything in sight—spectators, marchers, the decorations, anything she could think of that would make an interesting shot. She even talked one of the local merchants into letting her go up on his roof, from which she took several overhead shots.

The parade wound up with a brass band leading the final group of marchers, a group of descendants of Horace Brockenborough, the town founder. By now Randi had tired a little and was leaning against one of the police sawhorses. She didn't move from this position, but watched the parade through her lens, waiting for the perfect shot. That was how she first saw him.

First his father swam into focus. Mr. Taggert was a heavyset man, wearing a camel hair overcoat and a fur cap. With a sinking feeling, Randi realized that Ned might very well be marching as well, in honor of his descendants.

Then there was the flash of a red scarf as a familiar sandy head came into focus.

Chapter Eleven

Instinctively Randi's free hand shot up alongside the camera to try to block her face so that he wouldn't recognize her. This was getting to be a habit, she thought darkly. Why was she always hiding from him? Why wouldn't she give him a chance? *Because I don't want to set myself up to be hurt again*, she told herself.

But her scheme didn't work. Ned's gaze immediately focused on her crouching figure, as if by some kind of radar. To Randi's dismay, she could feel her face start to get hot.

Through the viewfinder she watched him break away from the other marchers and come toward her. Summoning up all her courage, she mechanically forced herself to straighten up and look at him. At the same time she pulled her wool cap down a little lower to hide as much of her scarlet face as possible.

By then he was in front of her. "I thought that was you," he said tentatively. It almost seemed as if he were afraid to talk to her.

"It's me, all right," Randi said bashfully. At least she hadn't stuttered. Despite her red face, the rest of her felt fairly calm. Maybe he would think she was red from the cold, she hoped.

Ned took his hands out of his pockets and cupped them to his mouth, blowing on them to warm them. "So what's happening?" he asked in a muffled voice.

"I'm taking some pictures," Randi replied, and then when she realized that was obvious from the camera hanging around her neck, she added, "for the *Clarion*." She couldn't believe she'd said it. Usually she was too modest to admit her accomplishments, but this idea was so new and exciting that it just slipped out.

"No kidding?" he replied with genuine interest, shoving his hands back into his pockets. "Do you mind if I hang out with you for a while? Maybe I could pick up some pointers."

"Well, the parade's almost over," she said,

looking toward the marchers retreating down the street and cursing herself at the same time. What was she trying to do, anyway? Get rid of him? *You like him, stupid,* she told herself. *Don't blow it like you blew it with Charles. Give him a chance.*

"Actually," he said in a deep voice, "what I'd like to do is talk to you. Ummm, alone."

"I d-don't . . ." Then Randi remembered her resolution. "All right," she said softly. Whatever it was he wanted to talk about, it seemed awfully serious.

"Over there?" he pointed at the statue of Horace Brockenborough in the park that she and Amy had photographed several weeks before. Randi nodded her head.

When they reached the base of the statue, Ned leaned against a nearby tree, his arms folded against his chest. Randi sat down gingerly on the marble base the statue was mounted on. She felt like she had been called into the headmaster's office. Ned looked so stern.

After looking around as if to make sure they had complete privacy, he took a deep breath. "What I wanted to talk to you about . . ." He paused, as if he couldn't think of the right words. "I don't know how to say it," he finally admitted.

"Whatever it is, you can tell me," Randi said quietly. "I'm ready to listen now." She understood this kind of uncertainty. She felt that way so often herself.

"What I want to know is . . ." he began. The next sentence came out in a rush. "Do you still hate me?" His eyes moved to hers searchingly.

"No. Of course not," Randi whispered, taken aback. "What makes you think that?"

"You always kind of avoid me now," he said, moving his eyes away again and staring at the ground. "Like I'm some kind of pest or something. Or like you're afraid of me. I mean, I'll leave you alone if that's what you want," he mumbled, "but I don't want to. I really like you, Randi."

"You do?" Randi swallowed hard. She mustered up her courage to get out her next question. "Why?" she said simply.

"*Why?*" Ned repeated, his brow furrowed.

"I mean, why me? You could have any girl in school, in the whole town, probably. Even Linda," she added meaningfully.

"I don't want Linda, I want you. You're not like the other girls at BP," he said slowly. "They play so many games. All they live for is gossip. They think guys are just for show—you know, who can get the cutest guy. You're not like that. I might not know you very well, but I can tell that much."

Randi felt her pulse quicken. He truly liked her. She realized how much she had misjudged him. "I really like you, too," she managed to get out. It was an effort to say it, but she had to tell him. And it wasn't hard to talk to him, she realized, if she just relaxed and told the truth.

"I was hoping you'd say that," he said, exhaling loudly. "But I wasn't sure. I really didn't mean to leave you alone for so long at the dance. But the other day in the parking lot . . ." he said, his voice trailing off.

"That was my fault," Randi admitted, hanging her head. "I didn't mean to be so rude. The truth is, well, I hate confrontations. I guess I'm just too shy sometimes."

"I know," he whispered. "That's one of the things about you that I like." He moved away from the tree and edged over beside her, crouching down. He picked up a branch that was lying on the ground and idly twirled it in his hands, as if he didn't know what to say next.

"It's really stupid to be so shy," Randi said, feeling more and more confident. Having a heart-to-heart talk with him was surprisingly easy. "That's the reason I'm having such a tough time with my class speech."

"That doesn't have to be a problem anymore," Ned said, slowly turning to face her. He brushed a stray wisp of blonde hair away from her face. "I still want to coach you. You'll be terrific. Is that okay?" he asked, moving closer.

"It's okay," she whispered, staring into his warm blue eyes. Randi held her breath and tried to memorize everything about that moment as if it were a photograph. She wanted to always remember how the park looked, with the sun shining in the clear blue sky overhead and the evergreens laced with snow. And she wanted to remember how, even though they were both bundled up against the chill, she could feel the warmth of Ned's arms as they encircled her. Randi let out her breath, and Ned tilted her chin with his hand and kissed her. All the doubts she had about him were erased in an instant. Yes, this was a moment she'd remember forever.

The next week passed in a blur of wonder for Randi. And as if finally being sure of Ned's feelings for her wasn't enough, her pictures of the Founder's Day Parade appeared at the same time in the *Clarion.*

Amy had insisted on meeting her at the newsstand in the town square the morning the paper was published. It almost seemed to Randi that Amy was more excited than she was.

"Gosh," Amy exclaimed, as she studied the front-page layout, her jaw dropping open. One of the overhead shots Randi had taken from the roof of Barnett's Hardware nearly covered the page. And prominently written along the border of the picture were the words PARADE PHOTOS BY RANDI HINTON. "Where did you take this shot from?" Amy demanded.

"The roof of Barnett's."

"Randi, it's *so* cool. Look," she said, opening the paper, "there are more inside."

To Randi's surprise, the *Clarion* had printed six different shots, including her favorite, the one of a baby all wrapped up against the cold, a tiny American flag clutched in her mitten.

Amy refolded the newspaper, a gleam in her eye. "I'm buying every copy," she said impulsively, and with that she scooped up the pile of papers and headed for the cashier.

As Amy handed the money over the counter, Randi shot her a look. "What are you going to do with all those papers?" she asked suspiciously.

"You'll see," Amy said, picking up the papers and walking out to the sidewalk. Then she began stopping passersby and giving the newspaper away, giving loud credit to the parade photographer. Although Amy was half fooling around, Randi could tell how proud her friend was of her, and it made her feel good. Although it was a little embarrassing, she realized that being embarrassed once in a while wasn't all that bad. It was a part of everyone's life. She was starting to learn how to handle it.

Randi and Ned spent a lot of their free time together in the next few weeks—but not all were dates in the strict sense of the word. True to his promise, Ned had begun coaching her for her speech. They met in Tunstall Lounge during study hall to practice, and Randi came to think of the lounge as their special place. That was where they had first met, the day after the photography reception.

For the first few days, the problem with their coaching sessions was a distinct lack of concentration. They were still getting to know each other, just learning to open up to each other. Randi's speech seemed dull in comparison to the boy she was crazy about.

Then one afternoon, with the speech only a week away, Ned decided to get down to business. "We have to get serious now," he said.

The setting sun cast such a warm, romantic light across the lounge that Randi didn't want to spoil it, but she knew he was right. Sitting up in her chair attentively, she searched through her bag. "I have my speech buried in here somewhere," she murmured. They had at least gotten far enough along for the first draft to be written.

Ned got up from the long mahogany table in the center of the lounge and began to pace. "The main thing to remember when you begin is to focus on speaking to only one person. You have to mentally block out everyone else. That keeps you from getting so nervous."

"Any particular person?" Randi asked.

"It should be someone you feel comfortable talking to. Someone you know . . . and trust."

"I'll pretend I'm talking to you," Randi said quietly, a faint blush warming her cheeks.

Ned's face lit up. "I was hoping you might say that," he murmured, and flushed a little himself.

Randi stood up, cleared her throat, and focused intently on Ned. "The Grand Canyon has not always been the tourist attraction it is today," she said, reading from her note cards. Her voice was full of confidence, clear and strong.

Chapter Twelve

The outfit Randi had selected for the day of her class speech—a pleated tartan skirt, a simple white blouse, and a delicate set of pearls that had belonged to her grandmother—was hanging on her closet door, and early that morning she studied it intently. Was it too plain? she wondered. On the one hand, she didn't want to be too noticeable. She didn't want to draw any more attention to herself than was necessary. But at the same time, she wanted to look good—for herself and for Ned. Looking good would give her self-confidence, Ned had told her.

Just the thought of him sent a shiver of delight through her. It was wonderful that they were dating, of course, but even better, she knew she was going to get through her class speech because of his love and support. He was a great person—and a terrific coach! She knew she was well prepared. If only she could decide now on the right thing to wear! Running her fingers through her hair, she decided to stick with her original choice. Then the phone rang.

It was Amy, sounding like she just woke up. "Are you psyched?" she murmured sleepily.

Randi was touched that her friend had gotten up early to call her. Amy loved to sleep late. "Here goes nothing," Randi said, crossing her fingers.

"But are you *psyched*?"

Randi thought of Ned. "You know, I think I kind of am," she said, smiling a little.

"Good!" Amy said approvingly. "I just called to say that Rusty and I are going to be sitting in the front to cheer you on."

"Thanks," Randi said. Amy and Rusty seemed even closer than they had been before, she thought with pride. *I'm glad I persuaded Amy to give Rusty another chance.* Then she grinned at the irony of that thought. "Will you meet me after third bell? So we can talk about how it went?"

"You bet," Amy agreed with a laugh. "You're going to see, though. It's going to be a snap. Easy as pie."

Amy's words echoed in Randi's ears as she dressed, then set off for school. She got there an hour earlier than usual. Ned had suggested that she might want to practice the speech alone in the auditorium to get a feel for the room, and Randi thought it was a good idea.

Still, her heart beat a little faster as Kearney Auditorium swam into view. Kearney was an impressive, elaborately arched building, the oldest on campus, and its faded majesty always awed Randi. Just seeing it made her heart skip nervously. But she knew there was no turning back now.

As she came closer, though, the whole thing didn't seem as scary as it once had. Somehow she knew she was going to get through it. The reason was simple—she finally felt self-confident. She had certainly come a long way from the person who stuttered through Jane Austen, and it was all because of Ned.

The auditorium was unlocked, the lights were on, and the podium set in place in the center of the stage. Randi strode down the middle aisle with determination, trying not to notice all the empty seats, seats that would soon be filled with students.

She set her notes down on the podium, then tugged it back a little so that the light fell directly over her shoulder. Then she practiced the limbering-up exercises that Ned had taught her, stretching her neck, then bouncing down to touch her toes. After shaking her arms vigorously, she inhaled deeply, counted to ten, and paused. The exercises seemed to have worked. She felt calm and relaxed as she looked down at her note cards. She began to read. "The Grand Canyon has not always been—"

". . . the tourist attraction it is today," a familiar voice backstage chimed in with hers. A moment later Ned's face popped into view, a mischievous grin lighting his features. "I hope you don't mind," he said, "but I knew you were going to have a practice run, and I thought you might as well have an audience."

"I don't mind," Randi said softly.

"Okay," he continued in a businesslike manner. "I'm going to go stand in the back, and I want you to speak in a normal tone of voice." He strode briskly to the back of the auditorium. "All right!" he finally said. "Go ahead."

Randi began her speech again, but he immediately interrupted her. "A little louder," he called out.

Randi raised her voice and concentrated on forming her words clearly and distinctly, another technique that Ned had taught her. When he called out "much better," she relaxed and focused on what she was saying. It *was* an interesting topic, she decided, and she tried to emphasize the most interesting points with her voice, yet another of Ned's suggestions.

After she had run through it twice to her satisfaction, Ned came back to the stage for a final pep talk. His words were interrupted when the bell over Monroe Hall rang, signaling the start of the school day. A nervous jolt shot through Randi involuntarily.

"You okay?" Ned asked, noting her reaction. Randi nodded bravely. "Just remember to speak up," he said. "When the room is full of people, the acoustics change. I'm going to stand in the back, and if I do this," he said, raising his hand in the air, "that means speak louder. Got it?"

"Got it." She gave him a mock salute and grinned up at him.

As his deep blue eyes focused on hers, all of Randi's fears melted away in an instant. They both hesitated for a brief, wonderful moment, but just as their heads moved closer for a kiss, the main door of the auditorium creaked open, and they immediately moved apart, embarrassed.

It was Mr. Harvey, their English teacher, who was in charge of the class speech program. "Good morning," he said brusquely, moving up the aisle toward the stage.

"Morning, sir," Ned replied nervously. "I've been coaching Randi for her speech, and we were just practicing," he added quickly.

"Very good." Mr. Harvey nodded, but when he looked at Randi, his expression seemed to change, and Randi thought it looked like pity. Mr. Harvey had witnessed her public-speaking ability before, in English class, and evidently expected a repeat of that miserable performance. *I'm going to show him,* she thought to herself. "Hello, Mr. Harvey," she greeted him boldly.

"Good morning, Miss Hinton," he said as he climbed up the short set of stairs to the stage. Mr. Harvey always introduced each speaker and announced the title of their speech. "Are you all prepared?" he continued, fixing her with a quizzical stare.

"Yes, sir," Randi replied, gathering up the note cards on the podium and stacking them into a neat pile. As she turned to take her seat, one of the note cards slipped from her grasp and fell to the stage floor. Ordinarily this would have mortified her, making her feel like a klutz, but today she was under control. As if she were a model on a fashion runway, she calmly bent over, retrieved the note card in a fluid motion, then glided over to her chair.

"Good luck," Ned whispered. "I know you're going to be great." He gave her a brief kiss, then headed for the back of the auditorium.

The first students entered the auditorium, and as they took their seats, Mr. Harvey leaned over to her and whispered, "Now there's nothing to be nervous about—"

"I'm not nervous," Randi cut in. It was amazing, but true. She thought of all the good things that had happened to her over the last month—how lucky she was to have met Ned, how proud she felt winning the photography ribbon and having her pictures in the *Clarion*. At last she seemed to be on her way to a new self-confidence, and it was a wonderful feeling.

But there was no more time to think about this, because the outside bell rang again, and all at once she realized the room had filled up and gone silent. Mr. Harvey got up stiffly and walked to the podium. "Good morning," he said to the assembly. Randi spotted Amy and Rusty in the front row, and Amy winked at her. "This morning's class speech is to be delivered by Randi Hinton," Mr. Harvey continued. "Ms. Hinton's subject is . . ." He paused and looked down at the index card in front of him. "The Grand Canyon and its development as a tourist attraction."

Shooting Randi a sympathetic look, he returned to his chair. Randi got up and carefully walked to the podium, feeling as if everything were suddenly going in slow motion, almost like a dream. This was the moment she had dreaded for so long, it was hard to believe it was finally happening.

Setting her notes on the podium, she looked out at the sea of faces opposite her. There seemed to be a restlessness in the crowd, murmured whisperings and rustlings, as if they were just waiting for her to blow it. Randi thought of something Ned had said. He'd told her that every speaker's first goal was to get the audience's rapt attention. She remembered his advice on how to do this: wait silently until everyone had settled down.

So she paused. Just as Ned had promised, the room finally went silent. Randi inhaled and began her speech. Out of the corner of her eye she saw Ned raise his hand, and she spoke a little louder. It was as if he were a conductor and she were the orchestra. The surprising feeling that this wasn't half as bad as she had anticipated came over her. She smiled.

As she continued, she pretended to be speaking to Ned alone, although she forced her eyes to rake the crowd. To her astonishment, they seemed interested in what she was saying. Gradually she saw heads move toward her in attention, and the rustling stopped, further boosting her confidence.

And then, suddenly, she came to the conclusion of her speech, and it was over. She collected her notes, overcome with relief, and blindly made her way back to her chair. Behind her, she was aware of the assembly's applause, but it wasn't until she sat down that she realized how loud and enthusiastic it was. It seemed to continue a little longer than usual, then faded away as Mr. Harvey got up to read several announcements.

Randi didn't hear a word he said. Her eyes moved from Amy, whose face was covered with a beaming grin, to the back of the auditorium, where Ned stood. He slowly raised his hand and made a circle with his thumb and forefinger. He mouthed a word at her, and she read his lips with a feeling of pride.

"Perfect." She couldn't believe it had been so easy.

On a warm Saturday afternoon two days later, Randi and Ned were strolling hand in hand through City Park, cameras slung over their shoulders. Randi had finally gotten around to giving him a photography lesson. It was the least she could do, she thought, after all the help he had given her.

"Your speech was so good that I think we should recruit you for the debate team," Ned was saying. He had been going on and on about this for most of the day.

"It's thanks to you," Randi said shyly.

"No, I think you have a natural ability."

"Well, let's not go overboard," Randi protested with a smile. Still, the idea of being on the debate team didn't seem as preposterous as it once had. But a lot of things, she realized, were different now. A little self-confidence went a long way. "Stand over there," she said, changing the subject abruptly. She pointed to a clearing where dappled light fell on a large rock. "I want to take your picture."

Ned obeyed sheepishly. "I hate having my picture taken," he protested, looking awkward and uncomfortable. "But for you . . ."

Randi remembered the picture that Vicki

Greene had taken of him and Linda at the Christmas dance and how that had nearly ruined things between them. It seemed so long ago. She realized with a start what a different person she had become since then.

Ned leaned against the rock, a serious expression on his face, but as their eyes met, that familiar warm look came over him, and Randi fell in love all over again. Slowly she clicked the shutter, capturing the moment on film.

"*Perfect,*" she said happily.

We hope you enjoyed reading this book. If you would like to receive further information about available titles in the Bantam series, just write to the address below, with your name and address: Kim Prior, Bantam Books, 61–63 Uxbridge Road, Ealing, London W5 5SA

If you live in Australia or New Zealand and would like more information about the series, please write to:

Sally Porter
Transworld Publishers
(Australia) Pty Ltd
15–23 Helles Avenue
Moorebank
NSW 2170
AUSTRALIA

Kiri Martin
Transworld Publishers (NZ) Ltd
Cnr. Moselle and Waipareira Avenues
Henderson
Auckland
NEW ZEALAND

All Bantam and Young Adult books are available at your bookshop or newsagent, or can be ordered at the following address: Corgi/Bantam Books, Cash Sales Department, PO Box 11, Falmouth, Cornwall, TR10 9EN.

Please list the title(s) you would like, and send together with a cheque or postal order. You should allow for the cost of book(s) plus postage and packing charges as follows:

80p for one book
£1.00 for two books
£1.20 for three books
£1.40 for four books
Five or more books free.

Please note that payment must be made in pounds sterling; other currencies are unacceptable.

(The above applies to readers in the UK and Republic of Ireland only)

BFPO customers, please allow for the cost of the book(s) plus the following for postage and packing: 80p for the first book, and 20p per copy for each additional book.

Overseas customers, please allow £1.50 for postage and packing for the first book, £1.00 for the second book, and 30p for each subsequent title ordered.

First Kiss

First love . . . first kiss!

A terrific series that focuses firmly on that most
important moment in any girl's life – falling in love for the
very first time ever.

Available from wherever Bantam paperbacks are
sold!